Hell for the Holidays

A 24/7 Demon Mart Christmas Special

by D.M. Guay

ISBN: 9781676321781

Cover by James at Goonwrite.com

This book is a work of fiction. Any similarity between the characters and situations within its pages and real places or persons, living or dead, is unintentional and coincidental.

Dear Nerd, Ray and Sid, Mom and Schmoo,
Yay. We got another Christmas together!

CONTENTS

Hi. My name is Lloyd Wallace, and all I want for Christmas is a real vacation with no demons, no monsters, no fights. Well, there's always next year, right?

CHAPTER 1

Ha. Take that, Scooter Stevens!

I jammed the second snow-filled red sock into the top of my snowman. Or was it the bottom? Hmm. I'd have to think about that, because technically my snowman was upside down. He was doing a handstand. The smallest ball, his head, was on the bottom, the largest on top. He had two sock feet in the air, and the weight of his body was held up by stick arms. He had a big charcoal briquette smile, because he was totally amped to be the first snowman in the history of the Hummingbird Acres Annual Christmas Snowman Contest to do a handstand. Because, hellz yeah, I had nailed it.

This guy was my crown jewel, although I admit he was the third snowman I'd constructed in the yard today. Hey, I was hedging my bets. I didn't want there to be any doubt that I deserved the "Best Snowman" trophy. The other two were by the sidewalk, one wearing my Dad's yellow Hawaiian shirt and a plastic flower lei, one in a grass skirt and coconut bra. The two of them held up a cardboard sign that said, "Florida or Bust."

I was officially a snowman Picasso. Yep. I was a genius.

No other yard was gonna have three undeniably clever snowmen. I knew, because I'd already taken a spin around the neighborhood to check out the competition. There were about twenty snowmen littering the street, all pretty standard. There was one "SnOSU" Brutus the Buckeye football snowman and a bunch of run-of-the-mill snow guys in ugly hats, with the usual carrot noses and second-hand scarves. Scooter had made a unicorn, but the horn had already broken off. I was sure to win.

I couldn't wait to see the look on Scooter's face. That bratty nine-year-old beat me last year. He built a snow sea monster and sprayed it green with food coloring. He'd made little green snow humps all over the yard, so it looked like his lawn was the ocean and the monster was swimming. Technically, I think that's cheating. It was a snow *beast*, not a snow *man*. But the adults were too busy oohing and aahing and pinching his cheeks, telling him he was "so creative" to care.

I wouldn't have minded so much if Scooter wasn't *that* kid. The one who's a total angel in front of adults but a horrific monster the second they weren't looking. Yeah, that kid. Trust me. I knew a thing or two about monsters, and that kid was a monster. He even sneered at me and flipped me the double bird behind all the parents' back right before they turned around to hand him his trophy last year. Yep. You're going down, Scooter. That's right. D-O-W-N.

Suddenly, a section of snow by my foot began to shake and rumble. "Aaaah!" I stomped it with my boot. *Monster! Monster!* "Die! Die! Die!"

I jumped up and down on the snow beast. What? So I was a little jumpy. You would be too if you spent forty hours a week manning a corner store beer cave that doubled as a gateway to hell. I'd seen some things.

I stomped and stomped until the snow fell away, revealing the black plastic curve of a Magic 8-Ball. *Ugh. Seriously?* It was my guardian angel. He communicated via Magic 8-Ball because he was too lazy to commute. He rolled and landed triangle side up. Of course. Always an opinion.

"Can you please not stomp on me? I'm working in here," the triangle said.

"What do you want?"

"To let you know it's bad karma to vow to destroy a nine-year-old."

"Yeah, well. You don't know THIS nine-year-old," I said.

"Be the grown up, Lloyd." Angel eight ball shook his triangle back and forth in the window, like he was tisk tisking me.

"Yeah. Whatever. So you're always telling me. What are you doing here, anyway? It's Christmas Eve. I'm on vacation."

Why yes, if you must know, I had twelve *paid* days off from the 24/7 Demon Mart. I didn't have to go back until New Year's Day. High five! No monsters. No zombies. No giant hell bugs. No smarmy succubi slinking to the Temptations Tavern. For twelve whole days. And, I was still making plenty of fat cash. *Pinch me. I'm dreaming.*

Now, if I could just ditch this nagging angel eight ball, Christmas would be perfect. "Don't you have somewhere to be? Isn't this a big holiday in Heaven?"

"Yes, it is. Which is why Heaven is unbearable this time of year. Jesus this. Jesus that. Oh look, isn't baby Jesus so cute. Enough already. We get it." His triangle dipped down, turned and reappeared. "Two thousand years of all about HIM. I swear, His birthday celebration gets longer every year. First it was Christmas Day. Then he created Advent, because we suddenly needed a countdown to His birthday. Then, He said, 'let's throw in Epiphany. Those three kings were so nice. I just love frankincense, hint hint.' So now I have to fly down and buy Him frankincense every year. Do you know how hard it is to find these days? They don't sell that on every corner like they used to."

He rattled, his triangle twirling around and around in the liquid. Great. Clearly, I had hit a nerve. This could go on all day.

"Then it was 'what's the harm in celebrating until Mardi Gras?' Now look where that's gotten us. The Christmas stuff is out before Halloween. Pretty soon we'll have one day a year when we're *not* celebrating Christmas. Okay, Jesus. You're the son of God. You were born human. You saved everybody's soul. We get it already!"

"All righty, then." I tried to find something interesting to look at somewhere else because this was quickly becoming awkward. "Are you gonna be okay?"

I was pretty sure I heard him grunt. "I'll be fine. I'll lock myself in my apartment and work overtime like I do every year. Your family seems like a bunch of delightfully godless heathens. That'll be a nice distraction."

Great. He was planning to hang out with me. So much for a relaxing vacation.

"All I want is one Christmas that isn't about HIM!" Angel eight ball shook, sending tiny arcs of snow bits flying up all around him.

"All I want is a Christmas without demons and monsters," and nagging angel eight balls. Ahem. But that last bit clearly wasn't gonna happen.

His triangle turned. "Well, Lloyd. Here's to hoping all of our Christmas wishes come true. Just don't hold your breath, because Christmas blows."

CHAPTER 2

Dad put another log on the fire. The flames kicked up orange, so high they looked like they were about to melt the stockings to the mantel. Giant flakes of snow gently fluttered past the window. I sunk back into the sofa, dry and snug and warm and smug in the knowledge that I would soon have another "Best Snowman" trophy on my shelf. The judging was tomorrow, so as long as we didn't have a warm snap and the snowmen didn't melt, I was a shoe in. Oh yeah.

"Don't get a big head, kid." Kevin was lounging on a pillow next to me. He was wearing an impossibly tiny four-armed Christmas sweater that was green and red striped like a candy cane. "You haven't won yet."

Well, crap. "What are you doing here?"

"DeeDee said you're having a party. It's Christmas Eve, right? Did I get the date wrong?"

I stared at him, deciding how I should handle this. Yes. I did tell DeeDee about the Wallace Family Annual Christmas Eve Party. But I did it in the awkward play-it-cool, cazh mention way guys do when they're crushing hard and would tap dance across the moon if the girl of their dreams actually showed up. Outside of work. To hang out when she wasn't obligated to hang out.

But, I'd made sure no one else was around when I mentioned it. I didn't mean it as a blanket invitation to all of Demon Mart, because dude. When work involved a hell gate, work-life separation was essential.

"Really, kid?" Kevin huffed. He crossed his arms and looked away. "Right. I see how it is. You invited her, but not me. After all we've been through? I thought we were friends."

Oh crap. He could zone in on my brainwaves, even during winter break, couldn't he? Dammit!

"Yeah, dumbass. I can. I'm returning your gift, by the way. Jerk."

"Don't be like that. I didn't mean it that way. I just thought—"

"Thought what? That the cursed talking roach has tons of invitations? Yeah, sure, kid. People are lining up to have me scuttle

5

across the cheese board at their cocktail party. I'm a real hit."

Kevin's voice was cracking up a bit. I squinted and looked at him closely. I swear I saw a teeny tiny tear streak down his cheek.

"It's cool. I'll head home. It's fine. My place is real festive now that the smoke smell is mostly gone. Oh, did I mention my dickhead roommates burned down my Christmas tree?"

His cheeks were wet, and he was sniffling. Holy crap. He was crying.

"They have no idea how hard I had to work to get a six-foot balsam fir into the living room. NO idea." The tears were streaming now, like someone had dialed up Kevin's cry setting to Niagara Falls. "It took me eighteen hours to string the lights. Eighteen HOURS. It's really hard to drag those things through branches when you're this small. Hurrr...hurrrr...hahurp hurp."

Hole. Ee. Crap. Kevin was at Defcon projectile cry. *Quick. What do I do? Think! Think!*

"Uh...Hey, Kev. Do you want some eggnog?" I asked. "The mix is from a carton, but it's actually good. Mom goes pretty heavy on the booze, adds some extra spices. I could make you one with Wild Turkey. You like that, right?"

Come on. It was Christmas. I wasn't about to cast a crying cockroach out into the streets. I wasn't a heartless Scrooge.

Kevin's head swiveled. He looked up at me with wet eyes, his bottom lip—uh—well, you know how this goes. Whatever the roach equivalent of a lip was, his was quivering. "Of course, I want eggnog. Chop chop, dumbass. Just add a Turkey float to whatever your mom's already mixed up."

I smiled. Now, that's the Kevin I know.

"Do you want a drink, Dad?" I peeled myself off the oh-so-comfy sofa.

Dad didn't hear me. He was looking out the window. "Boy, that snow's really coming down."

It looked like someone was pouring buckets of gigantic snowflakes outside the window. I could just make out the dark outlines of my neighbors—my competition—in their black snowsuits, putting the last touches on their snowmen.

"The weatherman said snowmageddon is coming. Ten inches or more overnight," Dad said. "Maybe we'll get lucky and the highways will shut down. Then the relatives won't be able to make it for Christmas dinner."

We could dream, couldn't we? Yeah. We were both secretly wishing that would happen. Seriously.

"Don't get your hopes up. Last time they said snowmageddon was coming, it turned into fifty degrees and raining. Did you set up the karaoke machine?"

I nodded. Duh. It was a Wallace Christmas Eve party essential. Plus, I was the only one who could figure out the cords. Parents and electronics didn't mix, trust me.

Dad looked back to the fire and sighed. That giant licking flame was a teaser. It was gone now. He had somehow managed to put the fire out, despite adding more logs and newspaper. He poked at the pile of things that were supposed to burn but weren't, puzzled.

"Yes, I do want a drink," Dad said. "Make it a double. I'm going to need it, because well, you know."

A streak of dread rippled across his face.

Yeah. I feel ya, man. In two hours, the house would be filled to the brim with family "friends." At least fifty people. We actually liked about six of them. The others? Not so much.

Mom had this old-fashioned hang up about etiquette. She said we *couldn't* have a party and only invite the people we actually liked. No way. We had to invite everyone we interacted with regularly, even if we didn't like them, because we'd had the party for so many years in a row that everyone *knew* we had the party. Crabby neighbors, snooty garden club ladies, all invited. Because if they weren't? That would doom us to an entire year of unpleasant, awkward conversations.

"We didn't understand." Mom said there's an entire secret world of women's social codes. And not inviting everyone to a party everyone knows you're having? No way. You may as well walk around with a scarlet M for "meany pants" pinned to your sweater. So, long story short, it's better if we suck it up and invite everyone. "One stressful holiday party makes the other 364 days of the year go smoothly."

Who knew if it was true. It made my head spin. Either way, I wish she'd throw no party at all than go through this. Because boy oh boy, this party stressed her out. A lot.

When I waltzed into the kitchen, Mom was buzzing around fretting. Every surface was covered in food. She had five crock pots dialed up to eleven, bubbling with the latest concoctions she'd unearthed from the *Taste of Home Christmas Magic* issue. I watched her move every carrot, so each was perfectly aligned on the veggie tray. Then, while cursing under her breath, she moved all the cheese cubes into a pyramid so perfect a pharaoh would be impressed. She then inspected every cracker, leaving only the perfect, intact ones stacked neatly next to the cheese cubes. She stress-ate all the broken ones. She had so many in her mouth her cheeks were puffed up like a hamster's.

As if a house filled with horrible guests weren't stressful enough, this was also the one night of the year Mom insisted that everything be homemade. I didn't know why. She hated to cook. She'd once set part of the kitchen on fire trying to bake gingerbread men. Even the firemen couldn't figure out what went wrong.

That was a fun year. All the guests had to stand outside in the cold while the kitchen and all the appetizers were sprayed with fire suppression foam. If you ask me, God was pretty clearly saying, "Step away from the oven, Jennifer."

Then there was the year Big Dan brought pot brownies, and my Mom took them right out of his hand and walked around serving them to everyone. She was so touched that Big Dan baked something, we didn't dare say a word. Three hours in, half the parents were high. An ice storm had turned Hummingbird Court into a skating rink and the sidewalk was so slippery, the stoned parents couldn't walk up the hill, out of the court, to get home. They just kept slip sliding back down the sidewalk into our front yard, where they lay laughing. On the bright side, no one could say the Wallace Family Annual Christmas Eve Party wasn't memorable.

"Honey, be a dear and turn off the oven. I don't want to overcook that beautiful ham Mr. Faust brought us."

"The *what*?" I suddenly felt like someone kicked my legs out from under me.

"Oh, you didn't know? He brought us a Honey Baked ham this morning. Delivered it himself. Boy, is he handsome," Mom said. "That was nice, wasn't it? Not many bosses these days do nice things like that. He sure is one in a million."

Gulp. He sure was. She had no idea.

"Can you open the oven and check on it? I don't want it to dry out. We might need to cover it in foil. Go on, then."

I moved cautiously toward the stove, my stomach filling with ice cold dread. Honey Baked ham, huh? I half expected it to be a trick, a face-eating, thirty-tentacled beast disguised as a ham, waiting to attack me the second I opened the oven. But nope. It was a ham. A cloud of salty sweet deliciousness wafted over me.

"Mmm. Slice me off a piece of that," Kevin said.

Aah! I jumped. He was on my shirt sleeve, breathing in the aroma of hot pig. *Dude. Don't do that. You scared me!*

At this point, I knew better than to talk to Kevin out loud in front of normal people. That could only end badly.

"Well, excuse me. I'm here to oversee the eggnog situation. You're taking your sweet old time, but Uncle Kev's ready to kick start this party. Don't skimp on the Al. Q. Hal."

"Fine." I huffed.

"What?" Mom asked.

Okay. I guess I wasn't smart enough not to talk out loud to Kevin.

"The ham," I said. "It's fine."

"Oh, good." Mom didn't look up. She was too busy artfully placing croutons on top of the salad.

Now that the ham was secured, I went to the drink station. Mom had a wheeled bar cart that she kept in the attic. For two days each year, it was stocked, locked and loaded with every type of liquor anyone could ever want. Christmas Eve and Christmas Day were those two days each year. Any leftover bottles were sent to the pantry to gather dust on December 26.

Honestly, there weren't many leftovers. The neighbors were thirsty, if you know what I mean. And so was I, frankly. Dude. Don't judge. Enduring this party, followed immediately by a full day with our awful relatives? Yeah. You'd drink too. It was like liquid pain killer.

I grabbed a plastic cup off of Mom's perfect stack, scooped some eggnog out of the punch bowl, then topped it off with Wild Turkey.

"Yeah. That's right. Keep pouring. Don't be stingy now," Kevin said. "You're doing good, kid. Looks delicious. Now hold it up here so I can take a sip."

I lifted the cup to my shoulder. He sunk his mouth into the egg foam. "Mmmmm. Mmmmmmm. Mmmm."

Lots of yummy noises came out of Kevin. When he lifted his head, he had a ring of yellow egg froth around his mouth. "Now that's what Christmas tastes like, am I right?"

Kevin took another drink. "Mmm. This vacation is looking up."

Mom looked at me. Kevin ducked, and I plastered on a quick, fake smile. I took a tiny nip of the eggnog, pretending it was mine. My lips burned. *Jesus, Kev! How can you drink this? It's strong enough to kill a grown man.*

"It's cool," he said. "Roaches are almost impossible to kill."

"So, what are you planning to do with your vacation, honey?" Mom smiled. "That was really nice of Mr. Faust to close the store for Christmas week so all of you could spend the holidays with your family. That's almost unheard of these days. Your Dad and I have to go right back to work the day after Christmas."

"Uh..." I stalled while I came up with a better answer than the truth, which was that I planned to do basically nothing for twelve days straight. Video games? Sleeping late? Gorging on cookies? Sounded like heaven to me, but Mom didn't like that. She wanted to see action. She needed to see me 'doing something' with my life. Blah blah blah. But it wasn't easy to make up excuses with Kevin whispering in my ear.

"You know why Faust really closes the store, don't you?" he said.

Uh, because it's Christmas?

"Yeah right. Under all that Christmas crap is another holiday. An older one: Yule. Why do you think we get twelve days off, not just one or two?"

I don't know. I don't really care, either.

"Well, you should care. Yule is dangerous, kid." He dipped his face into the eggnog and took another long deep drink. "Hot damn, this is good. Your Mom's a stone cold fox *and* she knows how to mix a drink. I think I'm in love. Woo. I've got a buzz already!"

Stop ogling my Mom. And what are you talking about? Yule is just another name for Christmas. It's all like birth of Jesus and stuff. That's not dangerous.

"Ha. Yeah yeah, kid. Tell yourself that. That's good PR putting a cheerful spin on an absolute shit show. Look. Long story short, Yule is when particularly disgruntled hellspawn are mostly likely to disrupt the rebirth of the sun. It also messes up the gates. They go all wonky. Especially the soul gates. You ever been to an airport at Christmas? That's what the gates are like. Understaffed and overbooked. You know how many sad people die this time of year? Tons. It gums up the works."

I blank stared at him. Come on. Did you catch all that? I didn't because I was busy nodding at my Mom, pretending to care about the gossip she was telling me. Something about a divorce and things we weren't supposed to talk about? Whatever. Give me some props. I was no good at this kind of multi-tasking.

Anyway, Kevin rolled his eyes. "If anyone wants to plunge the world into eternal darkness and chaos and unleash hell on earth? This is the week they're most likely to succeed. Solstice and all that. There are all kinds of nasty wandering around now that it's dark all the time. Plus, the angels are too busy celebrating Jesus' birthday to intervene. The world's on the brink of disaster every single second this time of year. Everyone feels it, deep down. Why do you think holidays are so stressful?"

Horrible relatives?

"Well, that too," Kevin said.

Ding. Dong.

Uh. What was that?

Ding. Dong.

Crap. That's the doorbell.

"Who could that be?" My Mom stopped cold, a look of absolute panic on her face. "The party doesn't start for two more hours. No one with any manners would show up this early. It isn't done."

Kevin shook his head. "Well, kid. What did I just tell ya? It's gotta be demons. They're always the first to come and the last to leave. They're a pack of dickhead party crashers. Trust me. Don't answer it."

CHAPTER 3

Mom made me answer the door. She was too busy stirring some thick white concoction that had been stewing in the crock pot all day. Dad was busy with the fire. He had managed to fill the living room with smoke and was wrestling with a log and an armload of newspaper.

I was in the front hall and I could hear voices, sharp, clipped, angry before my hand even touched the knob

"Boy. If that doesn't sound like angry Christmas elves on a Wild Hunt, I don't know what does," Kevin said. "You might wanna lock it and wait for them to leave. That's the safe bet. Seriously, kid. Don't answer it."

Gulp. I leaned in and peeked through the peephole. My gut dropped right into my shoes. *Oh no.*

"Who is it? Goblins? Dwarves? Demons? Shit. Tell me you didn't invite Morty," Kevin whispered. "That smarmy pervert drives me nuts."

"Worse," I said. "It's my family."

Yep. The relatives. I could see Mom's family. Grandma Mildred, Grandpa Eugene, and Great Aunt Edna. And Grandma Linda, Dad's Mom. Lord help us all. The four of them were already fighting, throwing elbows, jockeying to be the next one to lay heavy on the doorbell.

This might be a good time to mention that my parents' families were like gasoline and fire. It was never a good idea to have them anywhere near each other. Mom's parents and Great Aunt Edna were buttoned up, conservative, and I had never once seen any of them laugh. Oh, and they were incredibly judgmental. For some reason, they also believed they were classier than everyone else on the planet.

And Grandma Linda. Well, classy isn't a word any person would ever use to describe her. Tacky maybe. Loud and flamboyant, definitely. Fun? Sometimes. She was the match on the criticism gasoline that sprang like a fountain from Mildred and Edna. They gathered in one room only one day each year: Christmas. Let's just say Christmas dinner was an all-you-can-eat buffet of thinly veiled insults, barbs, awkward silence, and underhanded compliments.

"Demons. Called it," Kevin said. "Seriously. Lock the door and wait for them to leave."

Kevin must have zoned in on my brainwaves. I backed away, quietly, slowly, because mean old Great Aunt Edna could hear a floorboard with a desperate relative running away on it creak at thirty yards. "Mom! Mom!" I scream whispered.

"Who's at the door?" She poked her head out into the hallway, looking terrified. She had a wooden spoon dripping with some sort of sauce in her oven-mitt-clad hand. "Please tell me it's Jehovah's Witnesses."

"It's the grandparents. ALL of them." I full-on panic scream-whispered. Because, Dude. It was Christmas Eve. They weren't supposed to be here until two o'clock tomorrow. A single day in the same house together was enough. Trust me.

Mom's eyes went so wide they were full circles. Her bottom lip quivered.

"Great Aunt Edna is with them!"

Mom deserved to know just how serious this was. She dropped the spoon and covered her mouth with her oven mitts. Yep. She froze, like someone had hit the panic button on our life. If our house were a submarine, the red alert would be buzzing and spinning, blanketing the house in flashing light.

"What are they doing here? They aren't supposed to come until tomorrow!" She started pacing. "Oh God. Not now! Why tonight? What do we do?"

She looked at me. I looked at her.

"We could turn off the lights and pretend we aren't home."

It was the best plan I could devise under such intense time pressure. Mom actually looked like she was considering it. Then she remembered that she was a tragically nice person who always did the right thing. That, and the lights were on, so any idiot could see we were home. Dammit, Mom. Why couldn't she be mean for once? Her niceness was exactly why we hosted a Christmas Eve party—and Christmas Dinner—for people we didn't like.

"Uh...uh..let them in. Hurry up. Act normal." She grabbed a paper towel and began panic wiping the puddle of goo the spoon had splurped across the floor. "And give your Dad a heads up."

I tiptoed through the kitchen, around to the living room. "Dad."

He didn't turn around. He was too busy trying to get the fire to light. Because he'd managed to put it completely out somehow. He was wrestling with a long-snouted grill lighter. He couldn't quite defeat the child safety lock. "Why won't you light?"

"Dad." Gulp. "The *family* is here. Great Aunt Edna is *here*."

Great Aunt Edna was code language for all joy was about to be sucked out of the room forthwith.

He dropped the lighter. His shoulders slumped. He looked at the Christmas tree, glowing warmly. The lights—blue, red, yellow—sparkling on the tinsel. Fat old Gertrude—our blind, deaf, nineteen-year-old, three-legged, obese cat—lay under the branches, on the tree skirt, leg up, happily licking her butt.

Dad blank stared at it all, as if he was trying to freeze just one moment of absolute unsullied Christmas joy, so the memory of that feeling could carry him through the next thirty-six hours. I feel ya, dude. I really do. "Okay," he said. "I'm ready."

I nodded. I shook out my arms and legs. *Okay, Lloyd. You got this. You can make it through.* I stepped to the door and opened it.

"It's about time. Are you deaf? Didn't you hear us knocking? Here. Take this," Great Aunt Edna dumped a bunch of plastic grocery bags into my arms, then pushed past me like an eighty-year-old, ninety-pound freight train. She rolled a small, wheeled suitcase right over my foot.

Ouch.

"Take this to my room," she said. "Thanks to the weather, we have to spend the night."

Dear God. Noooooooooooooo!

And it only got worse. Because there were more relatives coming in behind her, all wheeling suitcases.

My Mom's parents came in next.

"Well, Lloyd." Grandma Mildred stepped in. Her lips pursed as she sized me up. "Did you gain weight? You look fatter than the last time I saw you. If you let yourself go now, think how terrible you'll look at forty."

"See? Demons," Kevin whispered in my ear.

Tell me about it. It felt as if all the warm happiness and contentment were leaking right out of the house.

Grandpa Eugene was on her arm. She was leading him in. He was nearly as deaf and blind as Gertrude, but he was the nicest one in the bunch. Old age had dulled his judgmental edge. He'd graduated from cutthroat business man, heartlessly stepping on competitors, to too old to care. Plus, he couldn't see or hear anyone anymore, and it was hard to knock people down a peg once you were too palsied to hang on to any pegs yourself. He tried to hug me but wrapped his arms around the coat rack. "How's my boy? What are you talking about, Mildred? He's skin and bones!"

"Oh, he's doing real good, Gene," my Grandma Linda hip checked Mildred out of the way with her ample, curvy bottom and planted her thumb and forefinger directly on my cheek. She squeezed so hard it was like she was pre-popping zits I was gonna get ten years from now. "Oh, you're so handsome. Just like your daddy. Do I have good genes, or what? Helloooo," She bellowed, putting one glitter-nailed hand to her cherry-red lips. "Watch out, ladies!"

My cheeks flushed, and she put a box on top of the plastic bags Great Aunt Edna had give me. "Be a dear and take this to the guest room. Don't let anything happen to that box. My Christmas hair is in there. I wanna look great!"

Christmas hair. Yeah. You heard that right. Did I mention my Grandma Linda wore wigs? Big ones. In fact, she was fluffing up the ends of her blazing auburn bouffant right now. It was a color that didn't occur anywhere in nature. Trust me.

Mom appeared next to me, fake smile newly plastered across her face. "Hello, everyone. Merry Christmas. We weren't expecting you until tomorrow. What a nice surprise."

Wow. Mom was laying it on so thick we were knee deep.

"Didn't you see the news, dear?" Grandma Mildred snipped. "Traveling on Christmas is such a nightmare. There's a massive snowstorm moving in tonight. Half the airports out west are already closed. It's only a matter of time before the Columbus airport shuts down, so we had no choice but to come early."

"But you don't...*fly?*" Mom said, slowly, confused. "You only live forty miles away."

Yep. They always drove here. And not even past the airport.

"Why take the chance, dear," Grandma Mildred said. She slipped off her coat, handed it to my Mom to hang up, then looked around. She frowned and said, "Well, I see you didn't have time to clean."

"Wow. She's a peach. I got a few ideas about which gate she might be headed through in the end," Kevin said.

Yeah. I'm right there with you, Kevin. Right there.

In fact, my Mom had spent the last three days scrubbing the house top to bottom, clearing the clutter off every end table, straightening every shelf, dusting everything that would hold still long enough. She'd cleaned so much that Dad couldn't find the TV remote or his Sudoku book. Mom had been following us around for days, erupting into tears every time we looked like we *might* drop half a crumb on the carpet. She could have scrubbed and repainted and hired thirty maids and Grandma Mildred would have found fault. That was kind of Grandma Mildred's thing. To her, criticism was a sport.

"Oh, don't listen to her. The house looks lovely, Jenny," Grandma Linda said.

Grandma Mildred shot poison darts at Grandma Linda with her eyes, as she watched her give Mom two *mwa mwa* cheek kisses, leaving traces of her bright red lipstick behind. Grandma Linda stood up, smacked her gum, patted her gigantic red bouffant, then unzipped her coat, revealing a low-cut V-neck polyester floral-print dress straight out of 1975.

"So, where's my baby girl Brooke? It's been too long since I've seen my favorite granddaughter."

Okay. For the record, Brooke was my sister. And she was Grandma Linda' *only* granddaughter. Brooke routinely rubbed the awesomeness that was her life and her accomplishments in my face. All. The. Time. So yes, it might seem petty, but I didn't want you to think for one second that she actually *earned* the title of favorite granddaughter.

"She's on her way. She's driving in from Cleveland."

"Cleveland? Uck. With two degrees, you'd think she would choose to live in a nicer city."

Awe, Grandma Mildred, in top form.

"She has a job at a very well-regarded, award-winning PR firm there," Mom said, fake smile looking more like gritted teeth at this point. "We're very proud of her."

"Oh, Jenny. Don't listen to old Millie," Linda patted Grandma Mildred—who by the way, was not one to use nicknames or any terms of endearment, ever—right on the behind. Grandma Mildred's jaw dropped, and she recoiled.

"Cleveland is wonderful," Grandma Linda said, arms waving in grand gestures. "Brooke will have a great time. You know, I ran into a few of the Browns linemen at a bar back in '97 and let me tell you, that was a night to remember. Love that city. People there really know how to show a girl a good time!"

"Oh yeah," Kevin said. "I like *her*. She's just trashy enough to be fun."

Kevin. Shut up! Seriously. Ogling my Mom? Bad enough. But I draw the line at grandmas.

"Oh, Jenny. Something smells delicious! What have you got brewing in the kitchen?" Grandma Linda clopped her cha cha heels right on down the hallway to go take a look. We all followed her.

Except for Great Aunt Edna. She was already in the living room. I caught a glimpse of her on the sofa. She had unearthed a skein of turd brown yarn and was knitting. Dad sat up stick straight next to her, painfully trying—and failing—to make small talk.

In the kitchen, Grandma Mildred surveyed the abundance of food on every surface, clutching her purse so tightly I thought it'd snap in half. "Really, Jennifer. This is too much food for one holiday meal. How much did this cost? It's wasteful. And why did you start cooking it tonight? It'll all go bad by dinnertime tomorrow."

My Mom stood there, wringing her hands.

"Don't listen to her, Jenny. You've outdone yourself. It's beautiful." Grandma Linda's plastic chunky bracelets clinked together as she moved from platter to platter, marveling at how good it all looked. "What time does the party start?"

Mom's eyes went wide as dinner plates. Wait. Was she shaking?

Grandma Linda lifted the lid on a crock pot filled with a black paste. "Mmm. What is this, bean dip? Is it Mexican? Oh, Jenny. You always go over the top to make an impression! Is your book club coming tonight? Those ladies are so much fun. What time does the party start?"

"Eight." Mom's voice was faint, weak.

"Party?" Grandma Mildred's eyes were slits. She was frowning so hard the deep wrinkle lines around her mouth went completely flat. That was saying something, because those wrinkles were Mariana Trench-level deep. "You didn't say anything about a party. Really, Jennifer. Feeding strangers? On a holiday? You shouldn't waste money on such frivolous things."

Oh snap. At that moment, a hidden family truth suddenly became clear. Grandma Mildred didn't know about the Christmas Eve party we had had every year for the past seventeen years. The plot thickened. It suddenly dawned on me that Grandma Mildred had never once attended the Christmas Eve party. Grandma Linda had and frequently. One year, she even drank so much eggnog, she passed out drunk in the flower bed by the back deck and woke up in the morning covered in a light dusting of snow.

Well, well. Mom didn't invite her own mother. Really, who could blame her? Grandpa Mildred was a shotgun loaded with insults, gift wrapped in a discount-store turtleneck and quilted snowman sweatshirt.

Linda's plastic hoop earrings clinked as she beelined toward the bar like a booze-seeking missile. "Ooh. What do we have here? Oh, yes! Jenny, you always make a good eggnog. Always delicious. Don't mind if I do!"

"Typical," Mildred whispered, loud enough so we all could hear, to Grandpa Eugene. "If there's a bar, Linda will find it."

CHAPTER 4

An hour or so later, Grandma Linda was completely hammered, attempting to wrestle the remote control out of a very offended, very uncomfortable, and joylessly sober Grandma Mildred's hands. Seriously. It was like the Gorgeous Ladies of Wrestling, only with chunky seventy-year-old grandmas. They were on the cusp of full-on cat fight, growling "let go" and "well, I never!" at each other.

Kevin crawled out from under the sofa cushion to watch. "I won't lie, kid. This is kinda doing it for me."

Zip it, Kevin. Stop it. Right now. They're my grandmas!

"I'm a roach. I'm not dead." He shrugged and kept watching.

Honestly, things had been so bad that I wondered if the fist fight might actually be an improvement on the evening. We'd spent the previous thirty minutes listening to Mildred and Great Aunt Edna recount every single ailment, medical procedure (In gory, step-by-step detail), illness and death that had befallen the people of their hometown. People we didn't know. Jesus. So depressing. Grandma Mildred and Great Aunt Edna talked about health the way old men talked about weather or baseball scores.

At least the fist fight had gotten them to shut up. Christmas Eve was already so bad that I wished Brooke were home. At least if she were here, the relatives would be too busy gushing about how great she was to fight. Yep. I never thought I'd say it, but this Christmas Eve was starting off worse than usual, and the party hadn't even started yet.

The big vein in Dad's neck was pulsing as he tried to reason with the fist-fighting grandmas. But it was too late for talk. Mom was nearly in tears. She'd disappeared into the kitchen twice already to "check on the food" which, by the flush of her cheeks, I was pretty sure actually meant "take a nip off the vodka bottle."

Grandpa Eugene sat upright in the wing-back chair, snoring like a buzz saw, completely asleep. He'd reached the ripe old age of fall asleep anywhere, anytime. I'd once seen him nap, dead to the world, in a chair while two screaming toddlers jumped up and down in his lap. A not-so-faint note of rotten egg smell formed a toxic cloud around him. Did I mentioned he'd reached the age of constantly farting as well? If Dad ever got the fire going again, remind me to aim Grandpa's backside away from the open flame.

Great Aunt Edna sat on the very end of the sofa, her perpetual frown darkening the room like a storm cloud. She was completely unamused by the spectacle unfolding around her. Her face looked like an old, dry apple. Wrinkled, spotty, and carved into a permanent scowl.

Click. Click. Click. Her knitting needles clinked together. Brown wool trailed over her polyester pants. She was darkening the world with yet another homemade sweater. I wondered who would be unlucky enough to wear it.

So, this is the part where I should tell you those plastic shopping bags Great Aunt Edna handed me when she walked in? Those were Christmas gifts for me and Dad. They were only gifts in the technical sense. As in, they were given to us. But not gifts in the sense of something given with love or consideration for the recipient. What was in the bag? Oh. I'm glad you asked. Homemade sweaters, knit by the gnarled bony hands of Great Aunt Edna herself, from the scratchiest wool on earth, likely harvested from the meanest, most bitter sheep on the planet. She had standards, you know.

Did I also mention that the wool was dyed the same yellow brown as diarrhea? No? And that Edna never bothered to ask our size, so the sweaters were so big and baggy, Dad and I looked like we were wearing cable knit trash bags. And not to be nit-picky, but this sweater was itchy. It'd already left wide swathes of angry red bumps every place it'd made direct contact with my skin. And no, I couldn't take it off. The annual Great Aunt Edna Christmas Sweater was a hardship we had no choice but to endure. Dad and I were obligated to wear whatever wool monstrosity she gifted us, all night. Because Aunt Edna made it. And it was bad karma to hurt an old lady's feelings. (According to Mom. I, however, was willing to take the chance.) We weren't allowed to take them off until she went home. God help us.

The fire had gone completely out, which was probably best for me and Dad, because we were both absolutely boiling. Did I mention the sweaters were super hot? Yep. We were roasting like man chestnuts wrapped in twenty pounds of wool.

But the dead fire was also why Linda and Mildred were fighting over the remote. Linda had set it to the channel that aired the burning fireplace, "for ambiance. It's classy. Relaxing. Isn't it?" she'd said as she drained another highball glass of eggnog and watched the televised flames lick the edges of the flat screen.

Grandma Mildred demanded we switch it to the news. "Put on the Weather Channel. We need to know if we're going to be snowed in. We could be TRAPPED for Christmas!" Mildred wailed. "You remember the Great Blizzard of '78. We could DIE!"

Mildred wished. She rejoiced in misery. I could already see her weaving the epic tale of being trapped with her family during the Great Christmas Eve Blizzard of Hummingbird Court. It would be an ordeal she bravely endured, and that all of us—only through her wisdom, thrift and prudence—triumphantly, miraculously survived. She'd be rationing the appetizers and casting out party guests like the crazy lady in *The Mist* in no time.

I stared out the window, watching the gigantic snowflakes flutter past, and fantasized about what normal families were doing right now. They were probably baking cookies, hugging and laughing and wrapping another homemade string of popcorn garland around the tree. Or giggling while lighting the fishnet leg lamp in their front window.

But nope. Not us. We were in the Christmas trenches, surrounded by relatives we would never be caught dead with in a million years if we weren't genetically linked.

Grandma Mildred must have gotten the jump on Linda, because the televised Yule log abruptly clicked to the local news channel. An aging, tan Ken doll of a man sat behind a desk, white veneers flashing as he tried not to look too happy as he delivered bad news.

"We are now expecting up to twenty inches of snow overnight."

Oh God. What if we really were snowed in with the grandparents *for days?* Just kill me. Right now.

"And breaking news: Thirteen inmates who were being transferred to a maximum security correctional facility have escaped," the Ken doll said, still smiling.

He looked absolutely delighted. Weird. Maybe he couldn't *not* smile? Too much Botox? Who knew?

"The men were recently convicted of murder, for a series of homicides orchestrated by a drug-smuggling ring. They carjacked and assaulted a man after escaping from a holding cell," he said. "They are traveling in a stolen black van that was last seen on a highway traffic camera heading northbound on I-270 near Cemetery Road."

Crap. That was one exit away from my neighborhood. That fact wasn't lost on Grandma Mildred.

"Really, Jennifer. I told you to buy into a classier neighborhood," she said. "Is the front door locked? Those convicts are practically on your doorstep! It isn't safe here. Nothing but low-class trash. Why didn't you move to Muirfield or Arlington when you had the chance? Those are nice *safe* places to live."

My Mom's angry wrinkle—you know, the one between her eyebrows that formed a deep number eleven when she was miffed—well, it dialed up so high it made a one hundred and eleven. *Holy shit.* Sound the alarm. I'd never seen Mom so mad. I didn't even know a one eleven was possible!

Mom grabbed the remote out of Grandma Mildred's hand and flipped it back to the yule log channel. "Mother." Mom's teeth were clenched tight. "It's Christmas Eve. Let's be thankful for what we have. We are perfectly safe. We have each other, and there is plenty of food."

I could tell Grandma Mildred was biting her tongue. Her eyebrows shot up, she lifted her chin and looked away, as if she were above it all. Then, her tongue cut loose. She whispered to no one and everyone, "Well, there's no *good* food."

My Mom dagger-eyed Grandma Mildred, then one by one, locked eyes with every single one of us. She didn't say a word, but her declaration was crystal clear. One look said, "We are going to pretend to be a happy family, and we are going to have a fucking Hallmark Channel, *It's a Wonderful Life*, *Yes, Virginia, There is a Santa Claus* picture-perfect Christmas so help me God, or I will kill you all."

It was a declaration of war. I had no doubt Mom would smack the eggnog out of our hands and turn any one of us out, alone, hungry, to face the snow, cold and certain death if we did not smile and gnosh and be nice. In short: Christmas cheer, under pain of death.

Gertrude, still under the tree, must have sensed the tension. She stopped licking her bottom, looked around at all of us, blind and confused, then squatted and peed, right on the power strip.

Zzzzzz zzzzzzz zzzzzz.

The tree lights sparked and fizzled, then burned out. A swizzle of smoke wafted from the outlet as Gertrude waddled away.

For a hot minute, my Mom looked like she was about to cry.

Ding. Dong.

Everyone's eyes shot to the door. Eight o'clock. The guests had arrived. Party time.

CHAPTER 5

Thirty minutes later, the house was absolutely packed. The Members of the Hummingbird Acres Garden Club, the neighborhood watch, the Charity Ladies' Auxiliary—plus husbands who'd rather be home watching TV—and all the neighbors in a twenty house radius along with their children, including that little jerk Scooter, were rubbing elbows and beer guts in the living room.

Scooter was trying to fish Gertrude out from behind the sofa, presumably so he could torture her. Thankfully, she had been smart enough to run. I wasn't too worried. She was so fat, she was wedged in there so tight I'd have to move the sofa to get her out. Scooter wouldn't be able to dislodge her, no matter how hard he pulled.

Mom's carefully curated, tastefully bawdy Christmas soundtrack of Dean Martin tunes was swinging cheerfully below the buzz of polite, but really really boring small talk. Plans for a new senior center. Food donation drives. Should we plant petunias or pansies around the neighborhood sign this spring? Blah blah blah. All to a steady beat of Grandma Mildred admonishing Mom every single time she took a sip of wine. "Really, Jennifer. Mother's shouldn't drink. It's low class." *insert side eye at Grandma Linda* "We raised you better than that."

This, of course, only made Mom drink more and faster. Jesus. No wonder Mom never invited Grandma Mildred to the party. She was Grandma Grinch. And no, her heart wasn't going to grow three sizes anytime soon. We'd been waiting years for that to happen.

I closed my eyes. *Dear Lord, deliver me from this terrible party.*

Then, as if He'd answered my prayers, the front door flew open, and ten ladies in matching red sweaters poured in. Each sweater had a white llama on the front wearing a little striped scarf. The ladies all wore reindeer horns and bobbing mistletoe headbands that were already slightly eschew. They had smiles so big they practically hit the neighbor's driveway. And every single one of them carried in two bottles of wine—one in each hand—with bows on the labels. Mom's book club.

Thank you, baby Jesus. Thank you!

And they were already half lit. *Yes! Party officially started!* I could smell the wine on their breath over the aroma of the fifteen cinnamon candles Mom had strategically placed all over the house. You're not surprised, right? Not about the candles. Duh. No proper Midwestern mom could resist a holiday-scented Yankee Candle. They loved those damned things. I'm talking about the book club. The entire planet knows "book club" is secret code for "Mommy's flimsy excuse to drink wine" club.

Grandma Mildred's mouth got even tighter when she saw all the bottles and all the festive drunk ladies. If there was one thing Grandma Mildred hated more than alcohol, it was fun. But at least now there were enough fun people here to dilute her cheer-dampening efforts.

Great Aunt Edna passed more subtle, silent judgment. She sized people up and down as they walked by, raising her eyebrows and huffing, silently signaling that they shouldn't dare talk to her because she was busy knitting and not interested in this holiday joy nonsense. At least she kept her mouth shut. Although I wished she'd stop knitting. Her brown wool sweaters were definitely not bringing joy to the world. Hark, herald angels. Stop singing and hide her damned knitting needles already!

The book club ladies poured into the living room, jumping up and down around my Mom, yelling, "Hey, girl, haaaay!"

Big Dan stepped in after them and shut the door. Big Dan was my best friend and son of Mom's book club bestie, Mrs. Miller. His size XXXL green sweater (there's a reason we call him *Big* Dan) had a teddy bear in a Santa hat embroidered on the front. His mom had pinned extra tinsel and some blinking battery-powered Christmas lights to the front. "This ugly Christmas sweater thing has gone way too far," he said. He looked completely defeated, devoid of all self respect.

"Yep."

"Yours is way worse," he said, surveying the bulky brown handiwork of Aunt Edna.

Sigh. Yes. Yes, it is.

"Where's the bar?" he asked. "We're gonna need a drink if we're gonna survive 'til midnight."

"Follow me."

We staked out a spot in the kitchen, next to the bar, but with a straight shot view of the front door and enough of the living room that we could safely tuck and roll if someone we didn't like headed our way.

Big Dan pounded his first eggnog like it was a shot. He held out his cup and said nothing as I refilled it. He immediately pounded that one.

And another. He had that hollowed out, vacant look in his eyes, akin to a war survivor. That forced-to-endure-relatives, forced-to-small-talk-with-normies look people had this time of year. We were in the holiday trenches. Santa shell shock.

Just then, Scooter whisked into the kitchen and started stuffing his mouth with cheese puffs. He pulled a squinty laser eye look at me and Big Dan, and we glared right back at him. "I got my eyes on you," Big Dan said to him. "Watch out."

Scooter's eyes went to slits, mouth totally stuffed, lips painted bright unholy orange with cheese dust, and he stomped out of the room, off to cause trouble and rub the cheese off of his fingers directly onto some upholstery.

"That kid is a total dick," Big Dan said. "Did I tell you we caught him peeing on our mailbox post this morning? He was spraying it like a dog. When we busted him, he said, 'I'm sorry Mrs. Miller. I just wanted to draw you a pretty picture.' And then he did this big innocent puppy eyes thing, all blinking and shit. Mom believed him. Not me. That kid is a straight up sociopath. We must destroy him."

"I'm right there with you." My thoughts flitted briefly to my pending snowman trophy. *Ha! Eat snow, Scooter.*

Big Dan had nearly drained another eggnog when the front door opened, and an angel stepped in. She was surrounded by a halo of giant snowflakes. She was so beautiful, she was practically glowing. Okay. It wasn't technically an angel. It was DeeDee. She'd dyed her hair cherry red for the holiday. She was wearing a white fake fur coat. She looked like a sweet, red maraschino cherry on top of a mountain of whipped cream.

She shook the dusting of snow off her hair and boots, then slipped off her coat and hung it on the coat tree. I took one look at her tight red sweater, and my heart kicked up a notch. I suddenly felt warm all over, and not the I'm dying underneath twenty pounds of boiling shit-brown wool hot. It was the OMG. She. Was. Beautiful. And she actually came to my party, warmth of sheer joy, holy crap, it's a Christmas miracle. My heart was soaring, fluttering in circles around the ceiling fan on little hummingbird wings. She came!

Big Dan saw her and immediately dropped his cup. The remnants of his eggnog splurped across the floor. "She doesn't live around here."

His jaw dropped when he saw her take one look at me, smile, then beeline straight over.

She handed me a flat box, wrapped in gold-striped paper, then threw her arms around me and said, "Merry Christmas, Lloyd!"

She kissed me on the cheek and said, "Go on, open it."

Big Dan still wasn't moving. His eyes were big as dinner plates. Yeah, dude. I know. A girl this hot paying attention to me? It was hard to believe.

I slid off the wrapping paper. She came, *and* she had gotten me a gift. Hot damn. The night was looking up.

Okay, full disclosure: I didn't buy her a gift. Dick move? Maybe. But don't judge until you hear the whole story. The no gift situation wasn't for lack of trying. I'd had a lot of ideas, but I didn't follow through because everything I came up with screamed "LLOYD IS DESPERATE!"

An engagement ring? Probably premature. Three hundred chocolate-dipped strawberries laid out in a heart? Maybe too much. Hiring an entire off-Broadway cast of Hamilton to sing "In your eyes," full on *Say Anything* style, behind me while I stood on her doorstep professing my love via cue cards like a cheap recreation of *Love, Actually*. Well, you get the idea. This was what happened when you watched too much TV. You stole gift ideas from rom coms. If that didn't scream "please, for God's sake, love meeeeeeeee!"—and not in a good way—then I didn't know what did.

I opened the box. Inside was a neatly folded, brand new "Who Farted?" T-shirt. Mine had been coated with the pus guts of a thousand-eyed octopus beast from the depths of hell. I had to throw it away because that shit doesn't come out in the wash, trust me.

"But you hate my T-shirts."

"I changed my mind. I like you just the way you are," she said.

Big Dan wobbled and went white. He looked like he was about to pass out. Okay, now I was offended. DeeDee actually liking me wasn't *that* hard to believe. Was it? Shut up. Don't answer.

"Do me a favor and put on the shirt right now. This sweater makes you look like a big poop emoji." She was staring at the brown wool abomination.

I slumped. "My Great Aunt Edna made it for me. I have to wear it until she leaves."

"Does she knit regularly?"

I nodded.

"She must be stopped," DeeDee said.

Yes. Yes, she does.

DeeDee shook her head. "Families are the worst," she said. "My parents showed up, unannounced, to inform me that they're staying at my house for seven days. I told them I was going shopping tonight so they wouldn't tag along. I had to get out of there."

"You should have brought them," Big Dan said. "Stick them with

Lloyd's grandparents for a night, and they'll think twice before they ever visit you again."

"Oh, it's best if they stay home. They don't mix well with other humans. The entire world makes them uncomfortable. They're super religious, so pretty much anything joyful in life is a sin. Jokes, music, alcohol. They're very *Footloose*," DeeDee said. "I love my parents, I really do, but I can't be alone with them for another minute."

"They can't be all bad. They made you," I said. Oh yeah, I was so smooth I was like a freshly Zambonied ice rink.

"Well, let's just say if I had cool parents, I wouldn't be a goth philosophy major," she said. "I'd be an accountant in a power suit. They've been at my apartment for two days, and I'm about to snap."

Suddenly, another rush of arctic cold air rushed through the house. Pawnshop Doc stepped in the front door and immediately stomped snow off his boots.

"I invited Doc. I hope you don't mind," DeeDee said.

Blup. That was the sound of my heart hitting my insole. First, Kevin. Now, Doc? This was rapidly starting to feel like an awkward office party.

"Oh, now I get it," Big Dan whispered. "She brought her boyfriend. You're friend zone. Phew. The world makes sense again."

What? Friend zone? Shut up!

But I couldn't blame Big Dan for assuming. Doc was a man ten, which was on display for all to see as he peeled off his winter coat to reveal a tight, bright red sweater. Even though it had a big green Grinch on the front, he still looked like he was about to deliver a strip-o-gram. Doc was tall and so buff his rippling muscles were pulling at the seams in an extra-large. He looked like the swoon-worthy hero in a Christmas romance movie.

He walked up to me. "Thank you for this Christmas event. I have nowhere else to go," he said in his usual forceful but calm voice with just a hint of vaguely Caribbean accent. "My family is dead. They died horrifically. I am alone in this world."

Well, then. There was nothing you could really say to that, was there?

Doc handed me a small rectangle. *Oof.* It weighed a ton. I'd say it was gift wrapped, but the paper was black. I just stood there, holding it. Frozen in fear. *Oh God.* It could be a box filled with demons spiders. It could be anything! This was the same guy who ran a pawn shop filled with cursed objects. Some packages were better left unwrapped.

"Open it now, new man," Doc said.

Yes. He still called me "new man." I didn't know how long I had to work at Demon Mart to get a new nickname.

Okay then. I didn't want to touch the package, but I did, because Doc was staring me down, waiting, and he wasn't the kind of guy you could put off. I unwrapped the paper, hands shaking, terrified, the entire time. It was a book. A red one with a leather cover. *Gulp.* It looked like a teeny tiny version of the books behind the counter at Demon Mart. That was comforting. Not. The title was branded into the leather binding. *The Pocket Guide to Monstrous Creatures and How to Subdue Them.*

Oh God. Nope. Hate it! This was going straight to the bottom of the dirty laundry hamper along with my employee manual.

"There are many pictures," Doc said. "Because you do not read."

Uuuuuuuuuuuhhhhh. That was the sound of all my dignity leaking out of me like a slashed tire.

Okay! Okay! All right, already! So I hadn't read my employee manual yet, okay? And they all knew it. Do NOT judge me. If I'd learned anything, it was that these monster manual books caused nothing but trouble. I mean, Tristan nearly unleashed hell on earth with one stupid poem! So, y'all need to drop it already. Some books are better off unread.

"Keep it close at all times," Doc said. "Put it in your pocket, new man."

I eyeballed the book. Uh. No way. I did not want this in my pocket. That was way too close to my downtown bits, if you get my drift. There were a lot of ways having a hell book in my pants could go south. I looked back up at Doc, who looked me straight in the eyes, no smile, and didn't blink.

"It is for your protection," he said.

Fine. I put the book in my pocket. Because I was more afraid of Doc than the book.

Just then, Grandma Linda waltzed into the kitchen. "Ooh la la!" Her red lips puckered. She eyed Doc from head to toe like he was a chocolate-covered cherry. "Aren't you going to introduce me to your friends?"

She winked at Doc, then sashayed, wide hips swinging, right on over to the bar. She leaned over, arching her back and sticking her behind out extra far, as she glanced over her shoulder and wiggled her eyebrows at Doc. Oh my God. Was Grandma in seduction mode? This Christmas couldn't get any worse!

Linda pretended to search the bar cart for a drink, but come on. Like she didn't already have the exact location of all the brands and bottles memorized? This was Grandma Linda after all. Bars were her natural habitat.

"I...uh..." I said. Mission: Deflect from the horny grandma at all costs! "Thanks for the book, Doc. That was really nice of you. But I didn't get you anything. You have all that cool stuff at the pawnshop, so I couldn't think of anything you could want that you didn't already have. Sorry."

Doc wasn't listening. He was locked in on Grandma Linda, who blew him a kiss as she clip clopped her cha cha heels and her V-neck flower print dress right on out of the kitchen.

"New man. You will gift me the bottle of rum and some time with the big-haired woman." Doc snatched the bottle of Bacardi off the bar and followed Grandma Linda into the living room.

CHAPTER 6

So, this was turning into quite the party. Mom's tasteful Christmas soundtrack—an alternating mix of bawdy Dean Martin ditties and respectable Josh Groban holiday fare—was long gone, replaced by the book club's Top 40 1990s boy band dance mix.

Right now, Backstreet was back, and everyone was dancing. Except Grandpa Eugene, who was still asleep, and Great Aunt Edna and Grandma Mildred, of course. They were busy hairy eyeballing the ladies who were hopping, wiggling, and drinking wine, because God forbid anyone has fun on Christmas Eve. Their eyes were as big and round as dinner plates as they watched Grandma Linda and Doc dance together, jiggling and bumping hips. Doc—rum bottle in hand—seemed to genuinely enjoy it.

Ahem. Me? Not so much. Doc and my Grandma?? This was shaping up to be the worst Christmas ever. "I can't watch this," I said.

"Are you kidding? I can't *stop* watching. Your grandma's got some killer moves. You get it, girl," Big Dan said, draining his tenth cocktail while tapping his foot. He did a quick hip-shop shoulder roll and began to sing. "Am I or—"

"Stop." I stared at him.

"What? I like this song. Mom used to rock out to it when she was driving me to preschool."

"Can't deal," I said. "I'm out."

I made a break for the bathroom but immediately tripped over angel eight ball. He was rolling around on the floor by the—unlit, thanks Gertrude—Christmas tree. He was rolling slowly, stopping and changing directions every few inches. Something was wrong. I picked him up. The triangle bobbed in the liquid, saying nothing. Well, that definitely wasn't normal. Angel eight ball always had something to say. "Hey. Are you okay? Are you in there? Do you need help?"

The triangle bobbed just below the surface for a few more seconds before emerging.

"Gabriel made me go to the office Christmas party. Self-righteous jerk. I should have stayed home. Someone accidentally left the prayer faxes out. I peeked. It was awful. You don't understand. Prayers are so depressing this time of year. I hate Christmas."

The triangle turned. It actually said <hiccup>.

Wait. "Are you drunk?"

"I may have accidentally pounded a goblet of communion wine. Or ten. You would have, too. That party was the worst. <hiccup>"

Okay, then. So I had a drunk guardian angel on my hands. How much farther down could today spiral?

The triangle turned again. "Goodwill toward men, my butt. It's either jerks praying for bigger flat screen TVs or wishing Aunt Edna would die so they could finally put a treadmill in the guest room. Oh no. Did I say that out loud? That was Mildred's prayer. Shoot. Did I say *that* out loud? Oopsie. Cat's out of the bag now! You walk over there and ask Mildred why she thinks her mean aunt is still alive. I'll tell you why. Because we sure as heck don't want her, and neither do the folks downstairs. NOBODY wants her, okay? She's that awful!"

A normal person might have been surprised by that revelation, but come on. I was eyes wide open about the quality of my family. I was hung up on another detail: "Did you say prayer *faxes*?"

"Yes! I know. We're hopelessly outdated. We stopped upgrading tech in 1987, because we didn't know if IBM or Mac would win, then we just never got around to it after." The triangle dipped and turned. "We've got tons of openings in the IT department, but you know how that goes. People have to die to fill them. Most of the smart techies are still too young to snuff it. Or, they don't make the cut, if you know what I mean."

"What about Steve Jobs?"

Angel's triangle stared me right in the eyes. "Anyway. Moving on."

"Well, you can't be too outdated if you're talking to me all the way from heaven."

"Don't even get me started. We've been using Magic 8-Balls since the 1950s. Don't you think I'd rather be in an iPhone? I'm dying to use a gif. Now put me down. Make sure I've got a view of Doc and Linda. We've got a betting pool on how this will play out. I bet twenty silver shekels that Grandma Linda gets to third base."

"Cut it out. She's my grandma!"

"She's old, not dead," angel said. "Just look at her. She's still got it."

I left him on the ledge of the bay window, facing outside to spite him, because dude, that was my grandma! He was just as bad as Kevin. Speaking of, where was Kevin? I scanned the room, then rifled around in my pockets, checked my shoulders. He wasn't there. Weird. It wasn't like him to lie low. Oh well. He was probably fine. Maybe he was passed out somewhere, drunk and happy.

I beelined to the bathroom. Not because I had to go, even though eggnog does go right through me. I went because it was a safe hideout. Mom kept an eagle eye on me at these parties, because she knew I hated them. She would notice if I disappeared for too long. If she found me in my room gaming? I was a dead man. If she found me walking out of the bathroom? No problem. So it was the perfect place to hide until my sugar plum visions of Linda bumping and grinding on Doc went away.

But, as soon as I got to the bathroom door, I knew something was off. *Brrr.* The air was arctic level freezing, like there was no heat at all in there. Aw, man. Great. One of the fat old husbands had probably dropped a nuclear deuce in there and opened the window to air it out. Ugh. But these were desperate times, so I took a deep breath, braced myself and went in.

I was right about one thing: The bathroom window was wide open. But the bathroom didn't smell, apart from the chemical olfactory joy of Yankee Candle's "Home for the Holidays" burning on the vanity. There was no old man either. DeeDee was sitting on the toilet tank, holding a red Santa sack on her lap.

Oh crap. I immediately looked away and backed out. "Sorry!"

"It's okay, Lloyd," she said. "Come on in and shut the door so no one sees."

I did. Because, dude. Alone together. Isn't this how those 90s rom coms end up? That's when I noticed her Santa sack was filled to the absolute brim with candy canes. Like dozens and dozens of them, packed in at all angles. She unwrapped one, then dropped it right out the window.

So, help me out here. That's weird, right? Do people unwrap perfectly good candy then throw it outside onto the ground? No? I didn't think so, but I didn't know many girls besides my Mom and sister, so I didn't want to jump to conclusions. It could be some viral Christmas fad diet. The sniff the candy cane but don't eat it way to lose ten pounds by New Year. What? I'd seen crazier headlines. Remember that sunshine on your butt hole health fad? Yeah. Me, too.

DeeDee then took one of those gigantic, fat, foot-long candy canes out of her purse. The kind that are too big to have a hook and just look like a nightstick of peppermint sugar? She held it out the window, and something snatched it right out of her hand.

Aaaaaaaaaaah! Monsters! I fell back against the wall and did a full Fred Flintstone panic shuffle on the mat before landing straight on my butt, smack on the floor. I rifled around for a weapon and came up with a plunger. I gripped the handle so tight I thought the wood would splinter.

"Relax," she said. "It's just Bubby."

"Relax?" My voice was a desperate cry squeak. "Bubby? Here? Oh God."

This Christmas party was getting worse by the second! I could just make out the outline of Bubby outside, holding that fat peppermint stick in his top two claw-tipped arms while he chomped down on it with his razor-lined mouth. In case you forgot, Bubby was a two-story-tall blue centipede who looked like he was made from blue raspberry Jello. Oh, and did I mention that, even though he seemed like an overall nice guy, he lived in hell? He was FROM HELL?

"What's he doing here? Get him out of here!" I squeaked. And I mean squeaked. It was a little embarrassing, but come on, I was panicking here. You can't rock a sexy man baritone when you're scared to death.

Bubby stopped eating and leaned in the window. He looked at me with his four white eyes, and they got all droopy and sad. Like, full-on puppy dog sad. Seriously, golden retriever gold-standard level puppy dog eye sad.

"I'm sorry, Lloyd," DeeDee said. "I know he shouldn't be out."

"What do you mean 'shouldn't'?" Woah boy. *Breathe. Breathe.*

"Okay, yes. I snuck him out before Doc put the solstice lock on the gate. Don't tell anyone, okay?"

Oh no. Room spinning. Life spiraling downward quickly. Can't breathe. This kinda sounded like DeeDee was breaking a rule, and it sounded like a big one.

"Are you all right? You look a little white."

"No, I am not all right!" Contraband hell centipede, in the suburbs, right outside the bathroom? Thank God the neighbors were all in here partying, because they'd all die of heart attacks if they caught sight of that. "How are we going to hide him?"

"Don't worry. I stole a hex out of one of the books. See that little baggie?" DeeDee pointed at some hippy-looking tiny leather sack on an impossibly long string around Bubby's fat jelly-roll neck. "The normies can't see him when he's wearing that. Gotta love those hippy crystals, right? Although they can feel the cold."

She looked out the window, up at the sky. "I think he might actually be making the snowstorm worse. I've never had him outside this long before, so I'm not a hundred percent sure it's him. But it's probably him."

"Dear God. Why?" Like seriously. Why?

"I'm sorry, Lloyd. I couldn't lock him in hell for the holidays. Bubby adores Christmas. The twinkly lights. The cookies. Hot chocolate with marshmallows. He loves candy canes. It makes him so happy. They don't have Christmas in hell. Obviously."

Bubby somehow managed to make his eyes look even sadder, and now he was whimpering at me.

"I wouldn't have brought him here if I didn't have to. Usually, Bubby stays at my place over Christmas break. We snuggle up and watch Christmas movies and have a great time. But my parents wrecked our plans. They showed up unannounced, and the gate was already sealed. We can't risk opening it to let him back in, not during Yule. He can't be in the apartment with unauthorized humans. Especially people like my parents. They're the worst. So we had to move to Plan B."

"Plan B?" What I really meant to say was WHY DOES PLAN B HAVE TO BE MY HOUSE!?!?! I SIGNED UP FOR A HELL-FREE CHRISTMAS!! And yes, I totally meant that as an all caps, old people Internet panic scream.

"I didn't have anywhere else to go, Lloyd. None of us do. Why do you think I invited Doc and Kevin? They don't have anywhere to go either. All we have is each other. See?" She cracked open the vanity under the sink. "If you haven't noticed, Demon Mart is like the Land of Misfit toys. None of us fit anywhere else."

"Huuuu uhhhh ha hurp. Huuuuu huuuuu huuuurp."

What the? I peered into the sink cabinet. A sound, like tiny sobs, echoed around the plumbing. There, perched on one of the spare rolls of Charmin, was Kevin. He was clinging to a gigantic cup of eggnog like it was a life raft. Somewhere along the line, he'd added a tiny Santa hat to his ensemble. It was shake-bouncing up and down as he sobbed. And I mean ugly cry level sobbing.

"Uh, are you all right?" I asked.

He looked up at me. "I'm a God damn ro...oh....oh...oh...oach."

And yes, he did drag out that one word for oh, about two minutes.

"I went to see my family for Christmas, and they sprayed me with Kill Em Dead. And it didn't kill me, so no, I am not all right," he snipped. "Huuuu uhhhh ha hurp. Huuuuu huuuuu huuuurp."

Um. Okay, then. I was really really sorry I asked.

"Normally, Bubby, Doc, and Kevin spend Christmas with me. We couldn't go to Kevin's house. His roommates are the worst. We didn't know where else to go," DeeDee said. "I thought it'd be safe to come here, but I can tell you're upset. I'm sorry. We can leave. We'll figure something else out."

I didn't say anything. I was too stunned. I had a sobbing cockroach camped out under the sink, a jelly hell centipede staring in the window, and a hundred drunk people partying on the other side of the door. This couldn't end well. But DeeDee had this look in her eyes I'd never seen before. Heartbreak? Sadness? Maybe a bit of both mixed together. She was zipping up her candy bag.

I wanted to send them all away because I was scared. But somewhere inside me, I knew DeeDee was right. We were the misfit toys. We'd been through a lot together. And, as hard as it was to admit, when it came down to it, these people—creatures? (Dude. Demon Mart needed to issue some guidance on what we're supposed to call each other.)—had my back. More so than some of the withered old branches of my actual family tree. Would Great Aunt Edna and Grandma Mildred slay a monster to save my life? That would be a hard no. They were probably only here so it wouldn't be completely out of the blue if they called up one day to ask for my spare kidney.

Deep down I knew what I had to do. I knew what the right thing was. Whether I liked it or not, Demon Mart wasn't just a job, it was a life. There was no vacation. It was 24/7, even during Christmas break. So, I stood up, smoothed out my horrible brown sweater, and made a decision. "Bring Bubby around back. We've got gingerbread cookies in the kitchen. He'll like those."

CHAPTER 7

I cracked the window above the kitchen sink and handed a stack of fresh-baked gingerbread men to Bubby. In the interest of full disclosure, they weren't homemade—refer back to the story about my Mom setting the kitchen on fire—and they weren't regular gingerbread men either. They were karate-chopping gingerbread ninjas. Mom procrastinated, so the bakery only had the silly ones left. That didn't stop Bubby from licking them right out of my hand with his blue prehensile tongue. So gross. He made an excited *blleepppppweee* noise as he crunch crunched them down to nothing. Yeah. I feel ya, dude. I'd eaten two already. They were delicious.

DeeDee was holding Kevin's drink, so any casual person walking by would think that it was hers. Kevin clung to the rim, taking sips and crying softly as DeeDee gently patted his back. Then, out of nowhere, DeeDee lifted Kevin and the eggnog to me and said, "Here's to Lloyd, for saving Christmas."

Her smile lit up the kitchen. Bubby blurped in agreement. Even Kevin gave me a thumbs up. Well, not exactly, but as close as a thumbless roach could.

This tender moment played out to the romantic soundtrack of the Humpty Dance. Go book club moms. But the sound of laughter poured out of the living room. My coworkers might actually be real friends, and for the first time tonight, I felt deep down that the holiday was looking up. This might actually be fun. I clinked my frothy eggnog cup against DeeDee's. Gently. Duh. I didn't want to accidentally mush Kevin. "Merry Christmas."

The warmth of holiday joy surged up inside me for the first time since the relatives arrived. So of course, that's when Caroline Ford Vanderbilt stepped in my front door, wearing a thick floor length black mink coat. She was even wearing a diamond tiara, like she was the frickin' Queen of Monaco.

Seriously, God? You couldn't let me have one full minute of

uninterrupted holiday joy? I had a drunk guardian angel, an inconsolable cockroach and a contraband two-story-tall hell centipede munching candy canes and gingerbread ninjas in the side yard. Throw me a bone here!

DeeDee took one look at Caroline and groaned. "Lord, deliver us from the Real Housewives of Dublin, Ohio."

Caroline Ford Vanderbilt waltzed right over to us, looked at DeeDee and said, "Don't bother taking my coat. I can't trust it with *the help*."

Yeah. Caroline said "the help."

And she said it exactly like you thought she would, like she was spitting something disgusting out of her mouth.

"It's worth more than you make in a year," Caroline said. "Besides, I'm not staying *here*."

And she said "here" like most people would say, "dumpster of flaming turds and garbage." She looked around, eyeballing the house, the food, the decorations, lips pursed, looking vaguely disgusted.

"If you can't figure out where to stuff that coat, I have some ideas," DeeDee said.

Caroline eyeballed DeeDee. "Excuse me? I will not be spoken to like this. Lloyd, go fetch your mother. Her party staff is out of line."

Caroline took one look at me—assessing my no-brand, homemade, shit-brown sweater—and definitely would have either frowned or raised her eyebrows in shock and disgust if her face weren't completely frozen solid by Botox. I'll bet you ten bucks Caroline and the newscaster used the same plastic surgeon. "Lloyd, fire this girl at once. There's no time to waste."

DeeDee started to laugh, and I'm not talking a giggle. She cackled, so loud and hard, Caroline took a step back, recoiling. "Oh, Caroline. That is so you." DeeDee moved to pat Caroline's shoulder, but Caroline did this smooth dip lunge before DeeDee's hand could make contact. "I don't work here. I'm a guest!"

"Dear Lord." She looked DeeDee up and down. Caroline's nose broke free of the Botox and wrinkled up like the two of us had instantly transformed into a gigantic steaming pile of manure. It only lasted a split second. Caroline composed herself, straightened her tiara, floofed her blow out and smoothed out her huge mink coat. "Well, not every party can be Country Club caliber."

She didn't miss a beat. "I am Caroline Ford Vanderbilt. President of the Charity Ladies' Auxiliary. And you are?"

"You don't remember me?" DeeDee feigned surprise. "I'll never forget you. How could I? You were sooooooo sweet to the paramedics when they carried you out of my store. How is your leg?"

DeeDee looked at her doe-eyed and blinked innocently.

Oh. Snap.

Caroline looked as shocked as someone with a chemically paralyzed face could look.

In case you've forgotten, Caroline Ford Vanderbilt was once possessed by an Internet cult pervert in our housewares aisle. After breaking her leg in ten places and vomiting thirty gallons of green goop all over me, she threatened the lives of two paramedics because they had to cut off her designer tennis shoe to save her. And this was *after* she was de-possessed. She couldn't even blame a demon for her bad behavior, so Caroline couldn't pull the class-act thing with us. There was no going back after your true colors had been laid bare so spectacularly.

But Caroline either didn't know that or didn't care. Her faux polite grin stayed put, her surgically altered nose tilted ever higher, ensuring she could look straight down it at us.

"Hey. Kid," Kevin lifted his face out of his eggnog. "Eerp."

Yep. That was a roach burp.

"Feed her another bun," Kevin said. "Maybe this time we can carb the bitch out of her. Heh heh."

Just as Kevin went face-first back into his drink, my Mom Cha Cha-slid into the kitchen. Gah. It was that stupid one-hit-wonder line dance from the late 90s. You remember the one, and you're welcome. Now that song's going to be stuck in both of our heads forever.

"Oh, hi there, Caroline." Mom's voice was sing-songy. Happy. Her cheeks were really pink, and she was swaying slightly. Okay then. Mom was tipsy. "I didn't see you sneak in. It was so nice of you to come."

Mom moved to hug her, but Caroline stepped out of the way, leaving Mom clapping her arms around air.

"As the Charity Ladies' Auxiliary President, the very least I can do is stop by to wish my many selfless volunteers a happy holiday. Why, the world depends on the vast swaths of nameless worker bees like you to keep at it, every single day. Someone has to do the thankless unpaid work that keeps society moving forward." Caroline said the words— obviously rehearsed and meant to be heartwarming—while baring her shark-tooth smile.

DeeDee leaned close and whispered in my ear. "That was a stunningly accurate assessment of our current economic system. She does know that when the revolution comes, she's going straight to the guillotine, right?"

I elbowed DeeDee, hoping to shush her. I failed.

"Let them eat cake indeed, Caroline," DeeDee whispered.

Caroline glanced around at the food. "Lovely party, Jennifer. Who did your catering? It's so...*rustic*."

"Catering? Oh, you're too sweet," Mom said.

I was pretty sure Mom was the only person in the history of the universe who had ever, or would ever, call Caroline Ford Vanderbilt sweet.

"I made all of this myself."

"Why, homemade?" Caroline's eyebrows flicked up and stuck there in surprise. Her polite grin held on for dear life as she tugged at the collar of her mink coat. "That's so industrious. Bless your heart."

Oh hell no. She did not just "bless your heart" my Mom. DeeDee had clued me in. In uppity lady code, bless your heart was a stone cold insult disguised as a warm blanket.

"Here, let me take your coat." Mom stumbled at Caroline with her arms out. "What do you want to drink? Let me make you something."

"That's sweet, Jennifer, but I really can't stay. I have another engagement. When your invitation arrived, sadly I had already committed to the Country Club's Inner Circle Legacy dinner. Did you know my family was one of the original founding members? More than a hundred years of good fortune. We've been so blessed," she said. "Which reminds me. A token of thanks, to add a touch of class to your party."

Caroline glanced around the room in disdain, just to make sure we knew she thought we needed some class. She produced a bottle wrapped in a red ribbon, from somewhere under the thirty pounds of dead animal fur she was wearing. It was a bottle of Veuve Clicquot champagne.

My Mom gushed. "Oh Caroline, this is too generous. You shouldn't have."

"It's nothing, dahling." And yes, she said it like she had suddenly morphed into a British aristocrat. Dude. Let me take a second to remind you we live in Columbus, Ohio. Okay?

DeeDee rolled her eyes so hard, I could practically hear them squeaking in their sockets. She whispered, "You know that's the champagne rich people think is trailer trash, right?"

My gut tied into a knot. This was the first time ever I wished DeeDee would be quiet. The faster we could get Caroline out of here, the happier we would all be. Thankfully, Caroline noticed absolutely nothing. It was as if DeeDee didn't exist.

"Now, I simply must get going. The roads are already a mess. So much snow! And you know how flippant drivers can be in weather. It brings out the worst in people. Why, I was accosted by a speeding van just one block away from your house," Caroline said. "It nearly ran me off the road! I didn't budge, of course. You have to put bad drivers in their place, you know. I barely escaped with my life."

"Aw, that's so sad," DeeDee said. "For us."

Caroline ignored her. "Your neighborhood watch should really crack down. Ordinary folks are so downtrodden these days. Desperation leads to so many ills, Jennifer."

She then glanced at her obviously expensive watch, which was encrusted with what were probably real diamonds. "My, look at the time. Once again, good work managing the volunteers. Keep those worker bees buzzing, Jennifer. Ta ta!"

My Mom walked Caroline to the door and waved goodbye as she stepped off the front porch into the flurry of snowflakes. For an instant, Caroline looked a lot like a hulking wild animal in the moonlight—a big, black furry silhouette stalking through the white snow. As soon as Caroline opened her car door, Mom closed the door, turned around and said, "Thank God she's gone. She's such a bitch!"

My jaw dropped. My Mom didn't say mean words about anyone. She handed me the champagne and said, "Put this in the refrigerator, will you, honey? Momma needs to dance."

Then she cabbage-patched herself right back into the living room.

"So do I." DeeDee pulled me along, too, right into the melee and immediately laid out some moves as she said she was too sexy for her hat.

Jesus, Mom. I know your friends like to party, but seriously? Right Said Fred? This song needs to die already.

But even Kevin was singing, perched on the edge of his eggnog glass, dabbing with his top two legs. Yes. It was hard not to be caught up in the joy of being rid of Caroline, so I decided to roll with it. I pretended to be sexy and did a fake walk the catwalk move, bottle of Veuve Clicquot still in hand. Hey. Give me props. It's hard to rock it confidently in a homemade turd brown sweater. That ain't easy. But it made DeeDee laugh, so I kept at it.

But my joy was short lived. Because Angel eight ball rolled right off the window ledge and into my shoe. And when I ignored him and kept on dancing, he rammed my foot repeatedly. Ugh. I picked him up.

"Look out the window. Now. <hiccup>"

I kind of had to do what he said, because if I didn't, he'd only make a scene. So I walked to the window, pushed a Christmas tree branch aside and looked out. Caroline's hundred-thousand dollar Porsche was in the court, wheels spinning, shooting snow. Her car fishtailed, going nowhere. At first, I was all 'ha ha' because Caroline's misfortune brought me joy. It felt nice to see karma in action. But then, I felt the happy leak out of me. Because she was stuck, and if she couldn't get out, we'd be stuck. With her.

"Lock the door. Whatever you do, don't let her back in," Kevin said.

He was on my shoulder, Santa hat eschew, swaying. Drunk.

DeeDee appeared next to me. "I second what Kevin said."

Reeeerrrrr. Reeeeerrrr. Reeeerrrrrrr. Caroline's tires spun. Snow kicked up behind them.

I shook the eight ball. "Why did you bring me here to show me that? Do you want me to be miserable?"

"Not her. Look up the block. Top of the court. Do you see that?"

Honestly, no, because the snow was coming down so hard, I couldn't see much of anything. The neighborhood snowmen were already knee deep in fresh powder. But if I squinted through the curtain of big falling flakes, I could see streaks of blue and orange light flickering at the top of the street, maybe a block and a half away? "What is that?"

I pointed at the strange colors, dancing.

"Is that fire?" DeeDee asked.

It sure looked like it. The flames licked the top of a big dark shape. I could just make out the outline of a wheel. A fat tire facing up. *Oh shit.* Something big, a truck or a van, had flipped over, and it was on fire. "Oh my God."

"I'm on it." DeeDee must have seen the wheels, too, because she fished out her phone and dialed nine one one.

"Thanks, angel," I said. "You probably saved someone's life."

But the ball shook in my hand, back and forth. "No. They're totally dead. But something went wrong. Look. On the ground, in the snow in front of Caroline's car."

Reeeerrrrr. Reeeeerrrr. Reeeerrrrrrr. Caroline laid heavy on the gas, digging herself even deeper into the white powder.

Kevin and I squinted out into the storm. Huh. Something was moving in the snow, dripping down the court, inching closer and closer to the front of Caroline's stranded Porsche. Something hot and angry had melted the snow into a trench, forming a thin steaming stream. Whatever it was, it was glowing red.

Uuuuuuuuuuuuuuuhhhhhh. Yeah, that noise? That was all my happy Christmas dreams turning to dust. Don't even tell me what that steaming stuff is. I didn't want to know.

"Doc musta screwed up the seal. Something got out. Oh man, I'm never gonna let him live this one down." Kevin swiveled around and yelled. "Hey! Baldy! Get over here. Stop screwing the pooch so you can see how you really screwed the pooch!"

"Did you just call my grandma a dog?"

"It's a joke, kid. Relax."

"No. I will absolutely not relax."

How could I, with a river of hot demon streaming toward my house?

CHAPTER 8

The hot, angry red stream took a turn near Caroline's front bumper, melting a tight circle around her car. Doc had, at DeeDee's urging, reluctantly joined us at the window. The bottle of rum was half empty.

"Way to muck up Christmas, Doc," Kevin said, clearly intoxicated. Because, dude. It took a lot of liquid courage to talk to Doc like that.

"Do not blame me, bug man," Doc snipped. "I sealed the gate. Nothing can get out."

Except for the two-story tall jelly hell centipede munching candy canes in my yard, but who's keeping track?

"There's a fifty fifty chance it's not demonic," angel eight ball said. "There is a truckload of dead guys on fire at the top of the hill. Keep that in mind."

"There's a what!?!" I couldn't help but yell. "Dead guys?"

"Quiet kid, geesh," Kevin said. "Act casual! Last thing we need is for all the Moms to freak out. We gotta keep the party rolling until we figure this out."

"Bug man is correct," Doc said, examining the mysterious red liquid.

"Yeah, I'm with Doc on this," DeeDee said. "We need to keep everyone inside and distracted while we check it out. We need to keep this party as normal as possible."

Said the girl who brought the hell centipede as her plus one. Woah boy. Legs feeling a bit like noodles right now.

"Guys." DeeDee's voice was flat. "Do you see what I'm seeing?"

I mustered some courage to look and immediately regretted it. The steamy red stream had melted a complete circle around Caroline Ford Vanderbilt's Porsche, right as her back wheels stopped spinning. And now, some sort of goopy red liquid was rising up out of the trench. It looked like smoke, but acted more like the gooey insides of a lava lamp. It licked the doors and fenders, pouring up up up until it stood six feet high in spots, a little shorter in others.

"Well, that ain't good," Kevin said.

We watched as the orangey-red rippled and rolled and coagulated.

Well, that was the best word I could come up with. Basically, the smoke was no longer evenly spread around the car like a see-though curtain. It had formed clumps. Thirteen blobs floating up and down in the air, untethered by gravity.

"Well, shit," Kevin said. "What do ya think, Doc?"

"This is not good, bug man. I am afraid I will have to wait to seduce the big fine woman."

"Please tell me you aren't talking about my Grandma," I said.

"I am, new man," Doc said.

And of course, as if she knew we were talking about her, Grandma Linda sashayed over, ran her glitter painted fingernail down Doc's cheek and said, "I know what I want for Christmas this year." She winked at Doc. "Come dance with me handsome."

Oh God. Lalalaalalala not seeing this!

"Lovely woman." Doc wrapped his arm around my Grandma's waist and pulled her tight against him. "I must assist my friends. I will ravish you another time. You will see me again."

Then he kissed her, right on the lips, and dipped her back like he was a duke on the cover of a dime store romance novel. Grandma Linda made a happy "woo-ooo!" sound.

I froze in horror. This can't be happening. Stomach churning.

Angel eight ball shook. "Great. I just lost twenty shekels. I hate Christmas."

Grandma Linda took the bottle of rum out of Doc's hand, straightened out her wig, winked at Doc and retreated into one of the many clumps of overweight husbands who refused to dance. She clicked on her small talk flirt mode and boom. Grandma Linda was back in action.

Not me. I looked up at heaven. Okay, the ceiling, and prayed. Well, more like questioned. "Lava lamp hell demons? On Christmas? Seriously, God? Are you kidding? Help me out here."

My pity party was quickly interrupted by a faint *tssssp tssssp tssssp* sound, like a reverse shush.

Tssssp tssssp tssssp.

Huh. That wasn't the music, unless Ricky Martin had suddenly added a whisper track to "Livin' La Vida Loca." Remind me to talk to my Mom about her playlist. It's like 1999 barfed all over Christmas Eve.

Tssssp tssssp tssssp.

I looked around. I didn't see anything. "Do you guys hear that?"

Probably not. They were busy staring out the window. Intently. Too intently. And not at the red and white lights—an ambulance—inching through the snow toward the burning van. They were watching the orange misty lava blobs churn and slither, creepy and random, all around Caroline's stranded Porsche. One of the shapes suddenly twisted down, as if it were looking into Caroline's car window.

Um. Yeah. Does that seem weird to you? Has a column of blobby smoke ever stopped to stare in your window? No? Yeah. Me either.

I swear I saw the outline of a nose, as if the blob had morphed vaguely into the form of a human face. "Did you see that?"

Tssssp tssssp tssssp. Great. That whisper again. *Gah! Can't deal. Not now. Can't it wait? Bigger problems. Hello!*

"Any ideas, Doc?" DeeDee asked. "They're taking form."

Each of the thirteen angry orange-red shapes around Caroline's car were looking more and more like humans. Gassy, ghostly, lava-lamp blob humans. They moved in closer to the car, leaning in, looking at Caroline through the windows. They had her surrounded.

Okay, it sounds petty, but this was the first thing that popped into my mind: I wondered if Caroline would even notice them. Would red angry ghost guys rank high enough on the social ladder to merit an acknowledgment? It really could go either way.

She must have shut her car off because the headlights flipped off and her brake lights went dark. I took one look at her back tires, bumper deep in snow, and my stomach filled with dread. Great. On top of the red angry monsters, we were stuck with Caroline until a tow truck arrived. In a snowstorm. On Christmas Eve. Lord, help us all. She might be here all night.

Of course, when I thought it couldn't get worse, it did. The red ghost demon guys started pounding on Caroline's car. Fists reigned down on the windows. Or tried to. Whatever these guys were, they weren't solid, because their bodies broke apart just like lava lamp blobs, floating up and away in pieces as soon as they hit the solid metal body of the car. They didn't do any damage. The blobs just floated back down and reformed into bodies.

"Phew-eee. False alarm, guys," Kevin said. "They're like demon farts. Nothing but gas in the wind. Can't hurt a fly. Problem solved. Somebody get me a refill."

He rattled his empty cup.

The gassy things didn't seem to realize they weren't threats, at least not right away. They changed tactics, trying to open the car doors. They tried and tried, and failed and failed, and this seemed to bother them. They moved faster and punched harder, but it was no use.

"They really really want to get inside that car," DeeDee said. "Don't they know Caroline is in there? Be careful what you wish for, guys."

Their blobby state of being must have sunk in, because now they seemed to be talking to each other about it. Blobby hands scratched gassy blob heads.

Gulp. Yep. Stomach tied in a bow. Knees wobbly. For sure. Strange otherworldly creatures? Bad. Strange otherworldly creatures working together on a plan? Disaster.

"We must get the mean woman out of the car," Doc said.

"No thanks," Kevin said.

"She will be safe in here. We can protect her."

"Uh, do you know who you're talking about?" Kevin said. "Let 'em have her."

"That attitude won't win you a ticket to heaven," DeeDee said.

Kevin glared at her. "Clearly that ship has sailed."

Angel eight ball nearly shook out of my hand.

"What?" I snipped.

"DeeDee's right. Karma is real. We're totally keeping track up here." The triangle turned. "You have to help Caroline."

"No way. I'm not putting my life on the line for that awful woman."

"Good deeds don't count if you only do them for people you love."

Did I mention Angel Eight Ball was a judgmental jerk?

"Heaven's whole purpose is to be judgmental," eight ball said.

Gah! I shook him, hard. He hiccuped.

"Wait. We're off the hook," Kevin said. "Looks like Caroline is rescuing herself."

Sure enough, the Porsche's door kicked open, cutting the orange creatures in half, their smoke bodies swirling away into the night sky. Caroline stood up, smoothed herself out, and slammed the door shut behind her. The creatures quickly reformed and surrounded her. Caroline was unfazed. She held up the hem of her black mink coat to keep it from touching the snow. The creatures descended on her, angrily throwing punch after punch, but Caroline either didn't notice or didn't care.

"Wow. They really don't like her," Kevin said.

"Who does?" DeeDee asked.

Caroline was enveloped in red angry, undulating blobs. The creatures dipped and dove and scratched at her. But they didn't so much as smear her lipstick or move a single hair out of place. Weird. The good news? Caroline was fine. The smoke blobs appeared to be harmless. The bad news? She marched right out of the angry cloud, through the foot-deep snow, back up to my front door.

Ding dong.

Great. Caroline saved, party officially ruined.

My Dad was the poor sucker who let her back in. He had just stepped out of the bathroom and didn't know what kind of monster was waiting on the other side of the door. You should have seen the look on his face. He saw her there and his bottom lip quivered, his eyes went wide. He had no idea what to do or say, but it didn't matter. Caroline shooed him out of the way, clearly annoyed that she was stuck at our house and wouldn't be hobnobbing with the Country Club crowd anytime soon. "Be a dear and take my coat somewhere safe where it won't get stolen," she said to Dad, as she eyeballed DeeDee and slid out of her husk of dead mink.

I wanted to say, "Listen lady, we aren't happy to spend Christmas Eve with you, either," but I kept my mouth shut because my Mom raised me right.

DeeDee tugged on my sleeve. "Look."

She pointed out the window. The gassy red ghost demon dudes were moving toward the house.

Oh God. Night getting worse. Much much worse. I never thought I'd say this, but I had bigger problems than Caroline Ford Vanderbilt.

"Relax, guys. I've got this." DeeDee grabbed the bottle of Veuve Clicquot out of my hand. A moment later, DeeDee took Caroline by the arm and whisked her toward the kitchen, telling her, "I'm so glad you're staying. Let me pop open this wonderful champagne you brought us. A snowed-in car shouldn't keep you from celebrating. You deserve a lovely holiday."

In the kitchen, I heard the POP of a champagne cork and the slide of a window moving in its sash. The fiery angry apparitions were in the middle of the lawn, billowing ever closer to the house. A moment later, Bubby appeared, blurping and splurping his blue Jello Jiggler body through the snow. He chucked three gingerbread ninjas up into the air. They appeared to be karate kicking the sky as they dropped, head over heel, from his pincer into his open mouth. And it dawned on me that DeeDee was a genius. She didn't just go to the kitchen to ply Caroline with overpriced champagne. She'd also set Bubby in motion, powering him up for a good fight with the holiday sugar high only a stack of frosted ninja gingerbread men could give.

Doc, satisfied that Bubby had the situation under control, stalked off to find my grandma.

Kevin and I moved more Christmas tree branches aside so we could get a clearer view of the showdown unfolding outside. Bubby had slugged and blurped between the house and the angry creatures. The blob guys had formed an orange line at the edge of the lawn, like bandits in a cheap cowboy television show. Bubby stood before them, towering two stories above the ground. He opened his dozen rows of claw-tipped arms. He arched his back. His claw mandibles opened, and he emitted a low buzzing *whir virrrrr whirrrrr.*

I knew that noise. It was his buzz saw teeth. Because underneath Bubby's four white puppy-dog eyes, he was a stone-cold killer. That *virr whirr* was the sound of his teeth. His mouth was like a razor-lined circular saw that could suck in and chop up offending hellspawn like they were ice cubes in a blender. I almost felt bad for the blob guys. They didn't stand a chance.

A shiver ran down my spine. Because no matter how sweet he was to us, Bubby was still a two-story-tall jelly centipede of doom. From hell. And to see his true nature, well, it was pretty scary.

Bubby stood straight up and opened his claw-tipped arms. He howled at the moon. A rumble came out of him that was so low and intense that it shook the house a little. The ornaments on the tree clinked together.

Tssssp. Tssssp. Tssssp. That whisper noise again. Ugh. Not now!

The orange guys looked at each other nervously. They leaned back, putting their bloppy arms up, preparing to defend themselves.

"Yeah. That's right. Better run, dickheads," Kevin said. "Heh heh. I love this part. They don't stand a chance."

DeeDee returned from the kitchen with an eggnog refill. Kevin crawled onto the rim.

"Oh yeah. Cocktails and a show," Kevin said.

"You should have seen Caroline's face. She wouldn't drink her own champagne. Called that one. I made her a Cosmo instead. She drained it like she was a sink. And, I'm pretty sure she popped a couple of Xanax when she thought I wasn't looking," DeeDee said. "Maybe it'll take the edge off, and she'll actually be fun."

Wait. "She did what?" Xanax? Are you kidding me? Hello! We had thirteen—which I'm pretty sure was *not* a lucky number—ghost blobs out in the yard, and now we had a drugged up Caroline?

DeeDee shrugged. "I know. We'll keep an eye on her. Who knows? Maybe she'll be nicer if she isn't so tightly wound. We've got no choice but to roll with it."

Bubby attacked. He lunged at the fiery orange creatures. Bending nearly down to the ground in front of them. His razor mouth was set to high. *Whir virrrrr whirrrrr whir virrrrr whirrrrr.* He moved in close and readied to suck them in.

"Showtime!" Kevin clapped.

I looked away. I couldn't watch. I'd once seen Bubby eviscerate a swarm of hell mosquitoes. The second they hit his mouth, they exploded into a cloud of guts the texture of pus and color of mustard. Don't get me wrong. I was grateful that he did it, but you can't unsee that. And I didn't need to see any more flying hell guts. Who knew what unholy goo was gonna squirt out of these guys?

Whir virrrrr whirrrrr whir virrrrr whirrrrr.

Man. Bubby must be giving it to them good. No way they would escape. He'd be sucking him into his razor teeth with the full force of three thousand vacuum cleaners any second now.

Whir virrrrr whirrrrr whir virrrrr whirrrrr.

The noise stopped suddenly. Phew. The day was saved. Hallelujah! It's a Christmas Miracle. Now, back to the party.

Or not, because that's when Kevin said, "Well shit. Anyone got a Plan B?"

CHAPTER 9

"That went over like a fart in church," Kevin said, staring intently out the window as Bubby scratched his head, confused, and the red blobby creatures reformed.

"What happened?" That's what I get for closing my eyes. I was a day late and a dollar short.

No one answered me. Angel eight ball rolled and stopped, haphazardly, still tipsy, around the ledge of the bay window.

"If Bubby can't get 'em, they aren't from hell," Kevin said. "What are they, then?"

Tssssp tssssp tssssp. This time, I knew exactly where that whisper had come from, because something was vibrating in my pocket. Get your mind out of the gutter. No, this was not a fun vibration. It was a scary one. It was that stupid book Doc had given me.

Tssssp tssssp tssssp. It vibrated harder. Pocket guide my butt. That thing had to go. I dug it out of my pants, dropped it on the floor, and jumped back like it was a spider. Did I mention I'm terrified of spiders and that hell is chock full of them? No? I yipped. "Get it away from me!"

I backed smack into the wall of unyielding muscle that was Doc. He picked me up and moved me to the side. He looked down at the book, which was hopping and rolling around on the carpet like a Mexican jumping bean. "You must appreciate the gifts the universe gives you, new man," he said.

"But it's moving. It's talking!"

Doc's brows furrowed. He picked up the book and held it out to me. "It speaks because I included the audio book. Because you do not read."

Okay. These people needed to let the reading thing go already. I wasn't the only one. I Googled it. Like thirty percent of Americans didn't read *any* books ever at all, okay? And I had extra incentive to steer clear. Would you read a book if you knew it might accidentally summon a demon or open a hell gate? No, you wouldn't. I stared at the little red book.

"Take it," Doc said. "It chose you."

"What does that even mean?"

"I did not choose your gift. Your gift chose you," he growled, then grabbed my arm and smacked the book into my totally not consenting hand.

The second it hit my palm, the book jumped and shook. Gulp. The pages ruffled. It whispered. *Tssssp. Tssssp. Tssssp.* Great. Just great. It didn't move when Doc touched it. Only me. And the book chose me. See what I mean? If that didn't scream "run away" or "swear off books forever" I didn't know what did.

"I think it's trying to tell you something," DeeDee said. Her voice curled up at the end as if she was unsure. She stared at it like it was a puzzle. Gee. How reassuring. DeeDee, Miss calm and cool in a crisis was unsure. How many warning signs did a guy need, here?

"Chop chop, kid. Open it. We don't have all night. Look." Kevin pointed at the window. The red angry smoke blobs were pressed against the other side of the glass, looking in at us. "Do it now, or things could go south real quick."

I looked back at the bored, rotund husbands. Grandpa Eugene fast asleep in the armchair. Scooter still trying to pull Gertrude out from behind the sofa. Grandma Mildred eyeing Grandma Linda with disgust. *Good deeds don't count if you only do them for people you love.* Crap. I had no choice. I couldn't let Christmas go to hell. Not literally, anyway. "Fine."

I steeled myself. I touched the tiniest corner of cover possible and flipped it open. The book laid itself out flat, then the pages ruffled and shifted as if an invisible hand was running along the edges. It appeared to be talking. Well, not exactly. More like the words on the pages were whispering off. Tiny voices rose from the pages. Okay, then. Cursed book. Errr. Audio book. The greatest Christmas gift I had ever received or would ever receive. Said no one ever.

Then the book pages stopped ruffling and fell open and silent. An airy whisper floated off the page "lemurrrrrrrrrr."

"You guys heard that, right?" I asked. I had to give the book props. I couldn't roll an r like that.

"Woah. That's some Harry Potter shit right there, kid," Kevin said.

"What did it say?" DeeDee asked. "Maybe it's trying to tell us what kind of entities we're dealing with."

"I don't know!"

They all stared at me.

"Seriously, kid. Do we have to spell it out for you?" Kevin said. "Tell us what it says. Geesh."

"Why do I have to do it?"

"At this point, we all just want to know if you actually *can* read," Kevin said.

Gah. "Fine." I huffed, leaned over, and took a quick look at the page.

And I was immediately sorry I did. Worst picture book ever. There was a black ink drawing of a ghastly man, a ghost with empty black sockets where his eyes should be and a wide open, suffering mouth. Frankly, the dude looked miserable. There was one big red word underneath.

"Speak up, new man," Doc said. "What does it say?"

"It says *lemurs*?" Huh. I looked at the word again. Yep. It said lemurs all right. Maybe the book was a gag, like a medieval joke book, because I was pretty sure lemurs were cute fuzzy bear things that lived in rain forests or something. Hey, I watched Discovery Channel. I wasn't a complete idiot.

"Let me see." DeeDee grabbed it and inspected the page. "Lemures. Not lemurs. It's Latin."

She looked at Doc and Kevin. "Does that mean anything to you?"

Just then, Bubby smacked through a couple of the red angry guys who had been trying to jimmy the window open. They blubbed apart and reformed behind him. Bubby tapped on the window, put his claw arms up and shrugged as if he were asking me, "What do I do now?"

I mouthed, "Dude. I don't know!" through the glass.

Doc was laser focused. "What else does it say, woman?"

DeeDee's brow wrinkled. She whispered to herself. I peeked over her shoulder. There was some tiny black print under the big red Lemur headline.

"It says 'ritus erit veteris, nocturna Lemuria, sacri: inferias tacitis manibus illa dabunt'."

Oh no no no no no! I grabbed the book out of her hands. What was she, crazy? "Don't read that out loud!"

Reciting this crap out loud had gotten us nothing but trouble. Was I the only one who remembered?

"Relax, Lloyd," DeeDee said. She snatched the book back. "It's Latin. It means..."

She ran her fingers under each word and said the translation slowly. "It will be the ancient sacred rites of the Lemuria, when we make offerings to the voiceless spirits.'"

"Now that's how you read a book, kid," Kevin said.

"How do you know that?" I asked, ignoring Kevin. I wasn't about to let a roach smack talk me.

"Philosophy major," she said. "Translating dead languages and knowing weird things is our jam."

Doc shook his head.

"What?" I asked. "What is it?"

He didn't answer. He stared intently at the floor.

Kevin looked at Doc. "You heard of them before?"

"Yes, bug man. Lemure," Doc said. "They are the souls who do not cross over because they do not know they are dead. They do in death, what they did in life."

CHAPTER 10

"So, they're ghosts," DeeDee said. "That's not so bad, right? Ghosts are, like, everywhere."

Uh, they are?

"They are not ordinary ghosts," Doc said. "They are more difficult to subdue."

Woah boy. Situation going downhill. It's bad, we're screwed.

"I read about this once," DeeDee said. "If we show them they're dead, they'll go away, right?"

"See?" Kevin mouthed to me, pointing at DeeDee. "Reading makes you smart."

Shut up! You're a roach not a rocket scientist.

"I may be a roach, but at least I'm not a dumbass," he said.

"That is the theory," Doc said.

It took me a minute to realize Doc was still talking to DeeDee about the ghosts and not commenting on my conversation with Kevin.

"If they aren't from hell, they're lost souls, and I'm guessing their bodies are up there with the ambulance. If they see the bodies, they'll realize they're dead and cross over. Problem solved," DeeDee said.

"It may work, woman," Doc said.

"Then let's go." DeeDee pointed at Kevin.

"Dude. I'm not going outside. It's freezing," Kevin said. "Plus, they don't make snow boots in my size."

He pointed at his many teeny tiny feet as if we needed the visual.

"Fine. I'll go alone," DeeDee said.

"What? No!" Oh man. The words just came out, didn't they? Because my horny man reptile brain knew if I ever wanted a chance with her, I had to be brave. "I'll go."

Full disclosure: I totally regretted saying that. Because the rational part of my brain knew I was a giant chicken. Bock ba gock. But I couldn't let her waltz outside into danger.

"You're sweet, Lloyd." She kissed me on the cheek.

Wo-oah. All blood heading south. Feeling dizzy.

"But you need to stay here," she said. "Your family will notice if you leave. Keep them safe and distracted. I'll get the ghost guys' attention and lead them away."

"But—"

"They can't hurt me. They're smoke," she said. "Keep the party going until I get back."

She sat Kevin and his cocktail glass on the window ledge. A minute later, she stepped outside, and the door slammed shut behind her.

"Come on, kid." Kevin stretched out his top four legs and cracked his...knuckles? Well, the roach equivalent. "You heard the lady. Let's mingle."

I picked up the glass, with Kevin perched on the rim, and waded into the crowd. Doc was back in party mode, bouncing Grandma Linda around as 'N Sync sang "Bye Bye Bye." I chose to ignore it and walk right on by by by, eyes forward.

"Ten bucks says Doc's gonna score. Heh heh," Kevin said. "Get it while it's hot!"

"Shut up, Kevin. She's my grandma!"

He shrugged. "I wouldn't kick her out of bed."

Kevin and I roll bounced through the laughing book club ladies and did our best to pretend there wasn't a hell showdown happening on the front lawn. I got my cheek pinched by my dancing, happy Mom. And, I caught Scooter standing on the sofa (with his shoes on, of course) bent completely over the back, still trying to dislodge poor Gertrude. Hang on, old girl.

"Kick him in the butt," Kevin said. "Kid's up to no good."

I was seriously considering it when Big Dan grabbed my sleeve and pulled me aside. "Hey. Bar's almost empty. We need to make a beer run, or this party's over. I'll drive."

"Empty? No way!" I said.

There was no way the bar was empty, and there was no way I was letting his drunk ass drive even if it was. But it wasn't. It couldn't be. Mom had stocked that bar to the brim, made gallons of eggnog, and the book club ladies had brought at least twenty bottles of wine. We couldn't be out of alcohol. It was only ten o'clock.

"Yes way," Big Dan said. "Look."

I followed him into the kitchen and sure enough. All the bottles were empty. Totally empty, not a single drop left, like they'd been licked clean. Empty wine bottles lined the counters, corks scattered on the floor. How the hell?

Suddenly, a green light flashed next to the eggnog. *Aaaaah!* I stepped between the bar and Big Dan so he couldn't see the small swirling green portal open right above the bar. A gigantic red hand with black claw fingernails emerged from the portal. The red hand put a bottle *back* on the bar. An empty bottle. Of tequila.

"Dammit. That's my stupid roommate!" Kevin yelled. He shook his fist. "They burn down my Christmas tree, and now they're drinking us dry? What a pack of assholes! Get a job already!"

Kevin was livid.

"How did he get *here*?" I screeched.

Kevin's roommate was always showing up at the store, hand poking out of portals begging for free slushies, but the store had a lot of gates. Why was this happening at my house? We needed to talk about boundaries. Work-life separation people!

"Well, I portaled over here," Kevin said.

I looked at Kevin. Kevin looked at me.

"Don't look at me like that. It's not like I can drive. I must have forgotten to lock the gate behind me. Sorry, kid. My bad."

Okay. So, now I was legit flipping out. But I couldn't yell, as much as I wanted to. At least, not out loud. *My BAD? Once the drinks are gone, the party's over! We've got a dozen angry lemurs and a hell centipede in the front yard. The party can't end now. No one can leave. What are we gonna do, Kevin?*

"Relax." he said. "I'm sure DeeDee's taken care of it already."

Big Dan said, "See? Told you the bar was empty. Should I pass some of these out? You know, keep the party going?"

He pulled a plastic-wrapped package of pot brownies partway out of his pocket.

"Put those away! Remember what happened last time?"

He shrugged and slipped them back in his pocket, but not before popping one brownie, whole, straight into his mouth. "What about the booze?"

"I'll take care of it. Go dance."

Big Dan shrugged, grabbed two handfuls of cheese curls, and shuffled back into the living room.

"Oh, you're gonna take care of it, are you?" Kevin said. "You gonna hold my roommate by the ankles and shake the booze out of him?"

"I don't know, okay? I just needed him out of here in case the hand comes back!"

Just then, front door opened and DeeDee stepped in. Our eyes locked. She stomped the snow off of her boots and raced into the kitchen. She wasn't relaxed. She wasn't smiling.

"Huh. She doesn't look happy," Kevin said.

Big Dan was desperately spooning the last of the eggnog out of the punch bowl into his cup when DeeDee grabbed my sweater, pulled me close, and whispered, "It didn't work. They wouldn't follow me. They wouldn't even look at me. And worse, I think they're up to something. The situation is a lot more serious than I thought. We need to keep everyone inside until we figure this out. Keep the drinks flowing while I go get Doc, okay?"

She looked at the bar. "Wait. Why are all the bottles empty?"

CHAPTER 11

Ironically, Kevin's dickhead demon roommate wouldn't touch the Veuve Clicquot, which sat open but full on the bar cart.

"I didn't know your roommates were so classy," DeeDee said.

"Trust me. They're not," Kevin said.

"Focus, guys!" I squealed. "What are we going to do?"

We were camped out in the kitchen and our Plan B brainstorming sesh wasn't going so well. Maybe DeeDee and Kevin didn't fully grasp the urgency. But seventeen years of Wallace Family Christmas Eve parties had taught me that as soon as the bottles ran dry, people headed home. And, call me crazy, I wasn't thrilled that the front yard was filled with angry blob ghosts and a two-story tall jelly hell centipede, even if normal people couldn't see them. DeeDee had said we needed to keep this party going at all costs, and that was what we were gonna do. But how?

Tink. Tink. Tink.

Angel eight ball was on the bar cart, lolling between the empty bottles, clearly still tipsy. "Oh Great. You're out of booze," the triangle said. "This night is going downhill."

Tell me about it.

"Maybe he can help," DeeDee said.

Angel eight ball immediately stopped moving and played dead, pretending to be a normal Magic 8-Ball, when he noticed DeeDee pointing at him. "Nothing to see here. Shoot."

The triangle flipped. "Better not tell you now."

I grabbed him. "Come on. The jig's up."

"Look. I don't get paid enough to angel two of you at the same time, okay?"

"Everyone knows you're in there," I said. "Help us already!"

I shook him, extra hard.

"All right. Stop! Stop! I'll do it," eight ball said.

"Blobby demon lemurs are trying to crash my party. What do we do?" I squeezed the ball, too tight. I mean, I was white knuckled on him.

"Well, we definitely can't let this party run dry. It's just getting good," eight ball said.

"I know that. But what about the lemurs?"

The triangle bobbed and turned. "Lemures. Big difference. You know, whiskey might get them to go away. Just a thought."

I shook him so hard I heard the triangle thumping against the plastic walls.

"Help MEEEEEEEE!"

"All right, already. Stop!" The triangle reemerged. "Cut me some slack! Man. My head's pounding. So much wine. I really let the smooth taste fool me. Stupid Gabriel. Stupid Christmas."

"Are you gonna help me or not?"

"I said yes, now put me on the bar."

I sat him down between the empty liquor bottles. He rolled a bit, still tipsy.

"Fill all these bottles up with water," angel eight ball said.

"You're kidding."

"Just do it. I've got this. <hiccup>"

Well, then. I wasn't ready to follow orders given by a drunk angel, because my confidence was not inspired, but DeeDee was already at the sink filling empty liquor bottles with tap water.

"The wine, too." Angel's triangle showed a line drawing of a hand, pointed at the bottles lined up on the counter. "Get to work."

"Fine," I huffed and started pushing all the empties closer to the sink. DeeDee and I fell into assembly-line mode. Ten minutes later we had eighteen wine bottles plus an entire bar packed with water-filled liquor bottles.

"Step back and let me work," angel eight ball said.

"So, what are you doing exactly?" I asked.

"Making you more wine. And rum. And whiskey. Now be quiet so I can concentrate."

"You're kidding. That's impossible!"

"Oh, I see how it is. Who do you think turned all the water into wine at that wedding in Cana? This guy." His triangle flashed a drawing of two thumbs pointing inward. "Angels do all the work, you know. God gets all the credit. Like every boss on Heaven and Earth. As above so below! Sometimes I think He only made us because He wanted to look awesome even though He sits around on His throne all day."

"I think you touched a nerve," DeeDee whispered.

"Now be quiet and stand back." Angel eight ball rolled, scooting some bottles out of the way to make more room for himself on the bar cart. I swear I could hear him grunting, like *grrrr. Grrrrt. Rrrrrt.* Awkward. Was he in the bathroom? Because he was kinda making the same sound an old man makes when he's honking out a dirt snake. Ya feel me?

Angel eight ball cursed. Then pep-talked himself. Nope. Confidence not instilled. If I were a betting man, I'd wager a disaster was pending.

"Come on, baby. Come on, you can do it. And...bam!" Angel said.

Suddenly, all the bottles were on fire. I screamed. DeeDee grabbed a dish towel and started smothering flames.

Eight ball's triangle turned. "Sorry. I accidentally hit Burning Bush mode."

The flames immediately simmered down to nothing, like angel had hit an off switch.

"Okay. That's better," his triangle said. "Here we go again."

Confidence definitely not inspired.

Grrrr. Grrrrt. Rrrrrt. "And, boo ya!" Angel eight ball said.

The bottles filled with beige goop that looked and smelled like...pudding?

"Oof. Sorry about that." The triangle turned. "Crack a window, will you? I hate the smell of tapioca."

"Are you kidding me?"

"I'd like to see you do better. Besides, I've had a few drinks." The triangle bobbed and turned again. "Now stand back. Third time's a charm."

"It better be!" I squeaked. Normally, I wouldn't have said it out loud, but I was feeling the pressure. Time was running short. DeeDee was behind me, chit chatting with people, stalling them, while subtly waving the smoke out of the room with a dish towel. Oh, man. Need booze quick! These people weren't lining up to pour themselves a festive glass of tapioca.

Grrrr. Grrrrt. Rrrrrt. Angel vibrated, levitating every so slightly off the bar cart. The bottles clinked and rattled. *Thud.* He dropped to the cart and rolled to the side, exhausted.

"That's it?" I squeaked.

"What do you mean 'that's it?' It's done, and it's top shelf. You're welcome."

I grabbed a wine bottle off the counter and sniffed it. Sure enough. He'd turned tap water into a strong Cabernet Sauvignon with a woodsy oak undertone. Yeah yeah. So I read that off the label. But good enough. I felt a ten ton boulder of dread lift off of me. *Yes! The day is saved!*

Or it was until Doc ran into the kitchen.

"Come quickly," he said, as a few of the book club moms managed to push DeeDee out of the way, because no one was gonna stand between them and an open bottle of Moscato. "Our friends are more clever than we anticipated."

We followed Doc through the squeeing crowd of Hammer-dancing mid-lifers—"Can't Touch This?" Really, Mom?—into the living room. When we got to the window, the red apparitions had surrounded Caroline's car and were once again attempting to break the windows and taillights, to no avail.

But all I could think about was Hammer time. Note to self: Ban Mom from Spotify.

"Man, those guys really hate sports cars," Kevin said.

"That's what they were doing last time," I said. "That's good, right?"

"No, it is not," Doc said.

Bubby stuck his face against the glass and started talking. Okay, well, talking in the way a lipless Jello hell centipede with pincers can talk. Anyway, we got the drift. He was desperately trying to tell us something, and it sounded kind of important. Bubby moved back and pointed. Huh. Now that I was really looking, only three of the blobs were attacking the Porsche. The rest were standing around the snowmen in the court, their orange glowing bodies blob drip dripping up into the sky then falling back down again.

They had my three about-to-be-award winning creations surrounded. Oh, hell no. No way. Back away from my snowmen, lemurs. I needed that trophy. *Need.*

Too late. While we all watched, one of the creeps burned a pencil-sized hole right into my upside down handstand snowman. And disappeared into that hole so fast it was like he'd been vacuumed in. Dammit! If he melted that thing, I was going to be really mad. Scooter had to go down. He *had* to!

The snowman shook. It was subtle, and I wouldn't have noticed it if a pile of new, loose snow hadn't shaken away from the socks. Oh, come on. Seriously? Not my snowman! I had to beat Scooter this year. You didn't even understand! These ghosts were jerks. I was on a path leading straight to a participation ribbon, and it was all their fault.

Bubby pointed to the Porsche. Huh. Now *all* the ghastly blobs were gone. And the eerie light around all the neighborhood snowmen? Gone. But don't dust off the high fives just yet. Because they had disappeared *into* the snowmen. And I knew this because a creepy orange light now illuminated the possessed snow creeps from the inside.

I watched in horror as my handstand snowman fell over onto his side. Then, my snowman sat up. His head swiveled, and he looked right at us with his beady charcoal briquette eyes and smirked.

Oh. Shit.

My Florida snowmen were moving, too. Swiveling their heads, looking around, motioning to the other snowmen on the street who were all now magically animated. Alive. Thirteen of them, including Mrs. Walsh's Brutus the Buckeye "SnOSU" snowman. Seriously. If you were from Columbus you'd think that was hilarious. Anyway...

Double. Shit.

Boy, these snowmen looked angry. Glowing orange. Charcoal mouths frowning. Snow brows furrowed and mean. They plopped and scooted and dragged their new snow bodies over to Caroline's car. They used their twig arms to crack the glass and dent the fenders, punching so hard bark was flying.

Holy crap. So much for harmless.

"Welp, this shit just got real," Kevin said.

Oh, yes, it did indeed.

"Woman." Doc turned to DeeDee. "What happened when you went outside?"

"They wouldn't follow me," she said. "I kicked a few of them and yelled, but they weren't interested. Some of them wanted into the car and the rest stayed at the window. They wouldn't budge. It's like they were looking for something, and I was invisible."

"This is not good," Doc said.

"You thinking what I'm thinking'?" Kevin asked Doc.

Doc nodded. They both looked somber and said nothing. And I did not like it one bit.

"Well? What is it?" It was better to tear this Band-Aid right off. Trust me.

"We might have vengeful spirits on our hands," Kevin said.

"What do you mean 'vengeful'?" I was trying really hard not to scream. But, dude. Totally panicking!

"Revenge," Doc said. "They have been wronged and seek remedy. We must find out what they want. We must know who they were in life. They will do in death what they did in life. They will not leave until they get what they want."

Doc grabbed angel eight ball, who'd been rolling around on the floor, following me. "Tell us what you know."

And, like a total dick, angel eight ball played dumb. Or dead. Something. His triangle bobbed, refusing to turn, stuck on that noncommittal thin line between replies.

"You cannot fool me, angel!" Doc was so angry, his eyebrows went from two down to one. "We need to know the hearts of these men!"

I took the ball. "Come on. Everybody knows you aren't a Magic 8-

Ball, okay? So start talking."

Triangle landed. "We've talked about this. For your eyes only, capeesh? <hiccup> You're the only one I'm getting paid to help. Now walk Doc back over to Grandma Linda. I need those shekels. I've got my eye on a new harp."

Jerk! I was in no mood for a lecture. "If you don't help me, I'll have a house full of dead party guests. That won't look good on your performance review, will it? Now start talking!"

I shook him. Really hard. Like really *really* hard. The triangle thwapped the plastic window, and the liquid sloshed so hard it got foamy. "Now, what the hell are those things?"

"Okay okay. Stop. Urp. Hold on. I'm going to be sick." The triangle sank. It reemerged a minute later. "Ugh. You do not want to see what just came out of my stomach. Don't ever shake the ball like that again. I might not actually be inside here, but I can still see what you're doing and you're making me dizzy. Do that again, and I will rain brimstone down on you. Got it?"

"Help me!"

"All right. All right. Relax. <hiccup>"

"Sober up already!"

"Easier said than done. I never should have let Gabriel talk me into that stupid party."

Gah! I shook him again.

"STOP SHAKING ME!" The triangle turned. "Look. I can't be a hundred percent sure, because I can't get the latest Hell Report until the office reopens after the holiday, but I'd bet the mummified head of Saint Catherine that flaming van up there contains the remains of the escaped convicts that were on the news earlier. The dead murderers."

"They're murderers?" Did it suddenly get hot in here? Did a mummified head just come up in casual conversation? *Vlurp.* A little hot bile tickled my tonsils. This might be the worst vacation I'd ever had.

"Figures," Kevin said. He took a big long chug of eggnog. Because of course, he was still hanging on to his cup. No way he was letting that drink out of his sight. "You don't get to be a vengeful ghost by living a happy life."

"Have either of you ever dealt with one before?" DeeDee asked.

Doc shook his head no.

"I did. Once. Back in eighty-four," Kevin said. "He was hard to put back, and he wasn't even a bad guy."

My legs went full on cooked spaghetti mode. *Hard to put back. Not a bad guy?* We had thirteen angry dead murderers on the lawn. Room spinning, to the sweet sweet sounds of Justin Timberlake. Shut up, dude.

Rock your own body.

"Does anyone have weapons?" DeeDee asked. "All I've got is a purse filled with candy canes. I didn't take anything from the store. I didn't think I'd need it. Doc? You?"

"No, woman," he said. "It is Christmas. We have only our wits to defeat them."

"Oh well, then. We're screwed," Kevin said.

"Maybe we don't need weapons. If they're vengeful ghosts, won't they go away if we give them what they came for?" DeeDee asked. "How did you get rid of the last one, Kevin?"

"Van Halen tickets. He died waiting in line for the show. Man, 1984 was a great album. Of course, we didn't know David Lee Roth was gonna quit the band right after. Shit, man. Van Hagar? Are you kidding me?"

"Focus, Kevin. How did you get him to go away?" DeeDee said.

"We let him watch the show. Front row seats. I mean, he sat on someone's lap, but he was a ghost so that guy didn't notice. He crossed over after DLR finished the encore," Kevin said. "He was a metal head, but these guys are convicted murderers. God only knows what they want."

"We must learn what they seek," Doc said. "Or we are all doomed."

Just then, a very intoxicated Caroline Ford Vanderbilt stumbled into the living room. "Merry Christmas, peasants." She raised a bottle of Wild Turkey. She had a fistful of empty shot glasses in her other hand. "It's been a terrible night. I was run off the road by a rusty van filled with disgusting working-class men. My Porsche is buried in snow. I should be eating veal at the Country Club right now, but I'm stuck with all you filthy hillbillies. Who wants to do a shot?"

I didn't know if the Xanax had kicked in or if it was the Christmas spirit, but something had put Caroline in party mode. She was intoxicated. And loud. So loud, in fact, that the thirteen living snowmen in the yard turned toward the sound of her voice. And that's when they abandoned the Porsche and started closing in on the house.

CHAPTER 12

"Wow. Relaxation actually made her worse," DeeDee said. "And to think all this time, she really was making her best effort to be nice. Who would have guessed?"

Surprisingly, Caroline's insulting declaration went over well with the crowd. As soon as she asked about the drinks, everyone cheered. The party goers descended on her. Glasses were held out. Caroline poured—and spilled—whiskey into all of them. Cheers were made, shots were pounded. The music and the laughter kicked up. Christmas Eve party in full swing.

Gee. If the house weren't surrounded by demonically possessed snowmen, I would have said it was the best Christmas Eve party we'd ever had.

"Why do they want revenge on the mean woman?" Doc asked.

"She has that effect on people," DeeDee said.

But as Caroline stood in the living room, barely able to stand up in her designer high heels—her sparkling tiara pinned into her two hundred dollar hairdo, frowning so hard it cracked her Botox—all the pieces clicked together. In Caroline's own words.

"I was accosted by a speeding van just one block away from your house. It nearly ran me off the road! I didn't budge, of course. You have to put bad drivers in their place, you know. I barely escaped with my life."

I looked out the window at the burning, overturned van. The red and white flash of the ambulance lights. At the angry glowing snowmen inching toward the house. They wanted revenge all right, on Caroline Ford Vanderbilt. She'd escaped with her life, but they hadn't. She'd run a van filled with escaped murderers off the road. The van must have flipped.

"She killed them all," I said.

Doc sighed. "A vengeful spirit will not rest until they have what they seek, and they seek the mean woman. They may seek her death as payment."

"I say we hand her over and be done with it," Kevin said.

Okay. Kevin said it, but we were all secretly thinking it.

"We cannot stand by and let angry spirits kill an innocent woman," Doc said.

So, maybe Doc wasn't on the same page then. Innocent. Caroline? Come on. That had to be one for the history books.

"We don't know they want to kill her," Kevin said.

"Vengeful spirits are in death as they were in life," Doc said. "These were murderers."

"Yeah yeah. I get it, okay?" Kevin said. "So what now? We've got no weapons. Nothing. And it's Yule. The angels are busy and no gates are gonna open up to help us. What's the plan?"

"Bubby." DeeDee wasn't suggesting it, so much as commenting on what was already happening. "Look!"

We did. Bubby was once again attempting to save the day. And he had really upped his game. I mean, he'd kicked into full Starship Trooper Klendathu warrior bug mode. (And no, I didn't read the book. I played the video game. And I don't want to hear another word about it, okay?)

Bubby reared back then came down on those snowmen with his sharp claw-tipped pincers so hard, he sliced them in half, straight down the middle. The snowmen split, and the halves fell flat onto the ground. High five, Bubby! Except. Dammit. No trophy for me this year. Fricking Scooter. I scanned the snow faces. The ghosts hadn't possessed his snowman. Snow unicorn. Snowicorn? Whatever. I couldn't catch a break, could I?

Eow! Something kicked my shin. I looked down. Speaking of Scooter. He was waist deep, on his belly, under the Christmas tree. Only his legs were sticking out. He threw kicks as he inched farther into the tree. He was after poor Gertrude, who had somehow managed to climb the trunk, inside the branches. I only knew this because I saw her hanging on for dear life behind some ornaments and string tinsel.

"Mew." Gertrude cried for help.

The tree was swaying. *Gulp.* If anything else happened to the Christmas tree, Mom would lose it. Her Hallmark Channel Christmas would officially go up in flames. I reached into the branches and grabbed Gertrude. I pulled. Eeeeh. Man. She was heavy! And she really had a death grip on that trunk, which was saying something for a cat with only three legs. (Long story. Let's just say she didn't look both ways before crossing the street, and it cost her.)

So there I was, attempting to wrestle Gertrude out of the tree, and I may have been kicking Scooter back a little every time he landed a foot on my shin. Maybe, just a little.

Suddenly, there was a loud, sudden *crrrrr* followed by the *tink tink tink* of glass shards raining down on the window ledge. This coincided with the Christmas tree falling over—hard. The tree hit the floor, and I stood there with a fat, blind, obese, three-legged cat in my hands. Gertrude flipped into full panic mode. She shrieked and writhed and clawed, leaving deep scratches in my hands and arms. Her claws even managed to punch through Great Aunt Edna's wool sweater, which was like a turd brown suit of armor. *Ouch!*

I put Gertrude down, and she was off like a shot. Honestly, I was impressed. I didn't know a cat could move that fast, let alone an elderly tripod who was so fat she was as wide as she was tall.

"Help. Help me." It was Scooter, calling from under the tree, which had fallen directly on top of him.

I won't lie. I was awash in smug satisfaction, and I was tempted to leave him there as punishment for peeing on the Millers' mailbox. *Karma IS real, Scooter. Ha!*

But everyone in the room had stopped dancing and talking, and was staring at the toppled, lightless tree. And at me, not helping Scooter, and at the twig that had broken the corner pane of the front bay window.

Well, poop.

My heart was thump thumping. Heat was rising in my cheeks. I was about to turn tail and run, like any self-respecting man, when my Mom stepped forward. But she hadn't seen it. Not yet, because she was looking at her phone. She said, "Oh no. Brooke isn't going to make it. The roads are closed because of the snow."

Then she looked up. Her eyes were pink and wet already, but when she saw the tree and the broken glass? Her bottom lip pushed in and out, and the tears started running down her cheeks. Yep. She was in full on Christmas cry mode.

Fuuuuuuuuuuu...

No one. And I mean no one, makes my Mom cry on Christmas. I had to save the day, at all costs. So I called out, my voice strong and loud over the thump of "Good Vibrations." Gah. Stupid Marky Mark. Stick to burgers and movies!

"It's karaoke time!" I announced, boldly and with a confidence I did not know I had. "We're doing it American Idol style this year. Vote for your favorite singer. Winner takes home two hundred dollars cash! The contest starts in the den right now. Go! Go! Go!"

CHAPTER 13

Boy, if you want to clear a room of drunk people in under five minutes all you need is a cheap karaoke machine and a grand prize. People love watching bad singers compete for cash. I guess that's why people like reality TV, right? Of course, I was gonna have to pay the prize money out of my Christmas bonus, because I'd totally made that up on the fly. But I was cool with that. You couldn't put a price on preventing your friends and family from getting eviscerated by blood-thirsty snowmen on a major holiday.

Everyone was in the den, safely tucked in the back of the house, away from the possessed snowmen clanking at the windows. The air was already saturated with the sour notes of a very high Big Dan butchering "Brown Eyed Girl." Jesus. He sang like a wounded antelope. Nope. He wasn't gonna win. Not even close.

I rolled the Christmas tree off of Scooter—I was feeling charitable —and shooed him off. Doc and DeeDee were at the window arguing about what to do. Bubby was pressed against the glass, his translucent blue body forming a jelly shield between us and the snowmen. I could see a couple of angry glowing snow creeps pressed against his behind. I guess he hadn't slayed those ones yet.

"You wish," Kevin said. He was tangled up in, and trying to free himself from, some brown wool on the front of my sweater.

I jumped. (Look. You never get used to the sensation of a roach crawling on you, no matter how many conversations you've had with that roach.)

"Maybe you aren't keeping up on current events, but we're getting our asses kicked," Kevin said.

"Wait. Did you just quote 'Aliens' to me?"

Kevin shrugged. "A. Classic film. B. Seemed appropriate. Anyway, Bubby sliced them all in half, but the bastards reformed again. You woulda noticed if you hadn't been messing with that kid."

What? No way! I ran to the window. I had to go up on tiptoes to get a clear view around Bubby's blue love handles. The remnants of two or three snowman were lying in pieces on the ground. Moving. The balls rolled around, collecting more snow. I watched them rejoin, building themselves into bigger, meaner snowmen. *Yep. We're screwed.* These guys looked like Terminator snowmen, for Christ's sake.

"Jesus hates it when people say that," angel eight ball said, lolling in slow circles on the window ledge.

"Not now!" I screamed. See? He always an opinion.

DeeDee had pulled the twig through the broken window. An angry snowman grunted at her from the other side. She'd taken his arm, and he wanted it back. His coconut bra was hanging on for dear life. My snowman had broken the window. And now it was trying to get in. Bubby was doing his best to hold the others back, to keep them outside of the house, using his body as a barrier.

I felt like all the blood drained out of me. The room was totally spinning. "Oh God. What do we do now?"

I asked, but no one answered. Because that's what DeeDee and Doc —and now Kevin—were arguing about: Plan B. Although, if you wanted to get technical, weren't we on at least Plan E by now? None of our ideas up to this point had been successful.

DeeDee suggested melting the snowmen, but Doc seemed to think they'd just transfer into some other object that might be scarier and more deadly than a snowman body. Like Caroline's Porsche. We didn't want the night to go full "Christine," with a demonically possessed car crashing through the front door.

I said nothing. Instead, I picked up the Christmas tree. Tinsel and ornaments jangled loose, plopping onto the carpet as I wrestled it upright and put it back in the holder. Then, I readjusted the tree skirt. Weird, right? Because never once in my life had I ever adjusted, or expressed any interest whatsoever, in a tree skirt. I did it because sometimes you need to go through the motions of normal when the world is falling apart around you. It's the busy work that holds off the hurricane. Apparently, Great Aunt Edna had the same idea, because she was sitting on the couch, knitting needles click clacking furiously, unleashing another turd-brown wool abomination on the world. She was completely oblivious to —or she didn't care about—the chaos around her. So was Grandpa. He was sound asleep in the lounge chair. Snoring. Still.

I had just tucked some tinsel around a branch when Kevin said, "I vote we throw Ms. Country Club Fancy Pants out on the street. Let 'em have her."

And DeeDee said, "Kevin. You're a genius."

CHAPTER 14

Fifteen minutes later, Plan B slash E was in action. The snowmen had scooted away from the windows. They were following the big black hulking fur-covered body of Caroline Ford Vanderbilt out into the court, away from the house. Hallelujah.

Okay. Full disclosure. It wasn't actually Caroline Ford Vanderbilt. It was her coat. DeeDee had filched it off the pile of jackets in the laundry room. (Technically, she stole it. Ironic. I know.) Bubby had slugged around the side of the house to the powder room window, which DeeDee had hung out of while she wrapped the coat around Bubby's behind. She had tucked and pinned and ruffled it, then made Bubby practice swishing it around, until we were all satisfied that he could perform a reasonable approximation of Caroline Ford Vanderbilt's snooty horse prance. At least, in the mind of a dead convicted murderer, who had possessed a snowman and was now seeing the world through charcoal briquette eyes.

In the meantime, Doc and I had held the angry snowmen away from the front window in classic Frankenstein style, with the threat of fire. It sounded cooler than it looked. There wasn't a Lederhosen-clad villager anywhere in sight. It was just me and Doc holding a lit Yankee Candle in each hand, waving them in front of the glass whenever a snow creep got too close to the bay window.

Doc and I didn't need the candles once Bubby's mink-clad behind appeared in the yard. The snow creeps turned and followed the hulking faux fur Caroline up the court, through the snow. They didn't seem to notice that there was a big blue hell centipede blubbing in front of it. Maybe because, for a gigantic bug from beyond, he was really working it. His mink-clad tail end sashayed and swung like lady hips. The rest of him was strutting, too, like he was popping it on a dance floor.

"Damn, Bubby." Kevin snapped his fingers (well..) and zig zagged his legs through the air. "Work it, girl!"

"We can't give them what they actually want, but we can make them *think* they're getting what they want." DeeDee said as she stepped into the living room.

She didn't seem to relish Bubby's performance like the rest of us. Her eyes were glued to that fur coat. She was wringing her hands, which made me nervous because DeeDee was kinda like a flight attendant. If you're on a plane and the ride gets bumpy, you know it's no big deal if the flight attendant isn't bothered. But if she looks scared? Well, you're doomed.

"These assholes must be dumb as a box of rocks." Kevin shook his head as he watched the snowmen follow Bubby's fur-clad tail around the court. "Guess that's why they're *convicted* murderers. Too dumb to get away with it, am I right?"

"That is not funny, bug man," Doc said. "People lost their lives to these men."

"Geesh," Kevin said. "Can't a bug make a joke around here?"

No one laughed. Because in a split second, the snowmen got the jump on faux Caroline. They rained down on her, stick arms swinging. They beat and kicked that coat so furiously, there was no doubt they intended to kill her.

DeeDee flinched. We all did. Bubby had his mouth covered with two claw-tipped arms, trying to contain the yelps of pain he surely wanted to emit. Because dude. For a bunch of snowmen, they could really hit. Hard. And they did, over and over, strangely in sync with the beat of Love Shack, which the book club ladies were singing together, badly, out of tune. Dude. If you're gonna karaoke, at least pick a song you know the words to. Just sayin'.

"Hang on, Bubby." A tear streaked down DeeDee's cheek. She grabbed my hand and squeezed it. So so hard.

Ow.

Doc stood behind her with his hands on her shoulders. "He will survive. He cannot die like us."

True, but it was still hard to watch. They batted Caroline's mink coat around like a pinata, Bubby's tail taking quite the thrashing underneath. A trickle of blue blood pooled in the snow.

A couple of the snowmen even high fived each other. Their charcoal frowns had turned upside down. Man. They were loving this.

Bubby tried hard to keep up the charade, making the coat look like a battered, wiggling nigh-defeated Caroline. He wagged the coat slowly, imitating her falling to her knees.

"I wish Ms. Fancy Pants could see this. She might actually die if she saw what we were doing to her precious coat. Heh heh," Kevin said. Well, clearly he was enjoying the show.

The farther Caroline fell, the more the snowmen's enthusiasm increased. Bubby dialed up the show, his fur-covered behind trembling. At last, he reeled up for his dramatic ending. Caroline's final death flop. But he hammed it up a bit too much because his tail flopped so hard on the ground the pins popped and the coat fell open, revealing the big blue jelly butt within.

Well, crap.

The snowmen looked at each other. They looked at the coat, and the orange glow inside of them turned red. Mean "Oh, hell no" red.

Fuuuuuuuuuuuuuuuuuuck.

Plan B slash E had failed. What the hell were we gonna do now?!?

"We need a better decoy," DeeDee said.

Then Kevin said, "You're about the right height, kid."

CHAPTER 15

Please, indulge a dying man's last wish and join me in a Christmas prayer. *clears throat*

> Dear Baby Jesus, protect me, for I do not want to die in drag. At least not dressed as Caroline Ford Vanderbilt. If I'm gonna go out dressed as a lady, please let it be with style. Like, RuPaul-level quality. For real. Thank you in advance for your heavenly consideration. Amen.

Yes. We had moved on to Plan F. Plan F for "Lloyd's fucked." And no, I was not being melodramatic.

DeeDee kissed me on the cheek and hugged me for a long time. "Be careful, Lloyd. Remember, if it goes south, Bubby's got your back."

"Yeah yeah. Cue waterworks." Kevin sat on DeeDee's shoulder as she prepped me for battle. "Hurry up. We gotta wrap this up before my buzz wears off."

"Okay. You're ready," DeeDee said. "It's time."

I hobbled, reluctantly, toward the door.

"Wait," DeeDee said. This is where I was a thousand percent sure she was going to tell me, "Don't go Lloyd! I love you, and I can't live without you!"

She actually said, "pucker up." Then, she fished a tube of bright red lipstick out of her purse and rubbed it on my lips. "There. Much better."

Before my cheeks had fully flushed pink from embarrassment, Doc pushed me out onto the front porch, then slammed and locked the door behind me. I stood there on the snow-covered all-weather outdoor fake grass carpeting, terrified. The wind was so cold I swear my eyeballs were beginning to freeze solid. Caroline's wet fur coat wasn't helping. The snow melted off of it when we brought it inside, and now the thing was drenched, smelled of damp rodents, and weighed a zillion pounds. Blech. Remind me again why rich ladies loved these things?

I adjusted my wig and stepped off the porch into the fresh snow. Yes. I said wig. Oh, did I forget to mention that I was also wearing Grandma Linda's spare Christmas wig in a bid to create a more convincing Caroline? It was a brown bouffant, and we'd stolen it out of her overnight bag. Don't ask me why she couldn't wear her red wig two days in a row, because I honestly didn't know.

I was also wearing the plastic rhinestone princess tiara and pink plastic glitter heels from Mom's Halloween fairy godmother costume. Yes. I looked like a bad drag version of Caroline Ford Vanderbilt, and no I wasn't happy about it. And if you tell anyone, I will hunt you down and destroy you, do you understand? Keep your lips zipped.

So here I was. Caroline Ford Vanderbilt 2.0. The new and improved decoy. And we'd really laid it on thick this time. Wig. Lipstick. Tiara. Fur coat. High heels. I also had a phone in my pocket loaded with clips of Caroline's voice. DeeDee had followed her around the party for ten minutes, recording everything she said.

The plan: Fool the snow creeps. For real this time. Let them think they have killed her. Let them see blood.

This is the part where I should also mention the mink coat—and Grandma's wig—were rigged with anything that could pass for blood. Fast food mini ketchup and Taco Bell Diablo sauce packs from the kitchen junk drawer, and corn syrup mixed with red food coloring twisted into tiny plastic-wrap sacs.

The idea was, after they hit me a few times, the blood sacks pop and make it appear that I am bleeding. Then, I play dead and hope they go away. This had to work, right? (This is the part where you say yes, we're geniuses, and it can't fail. Do it. Right now. I'm waiting. Hello...? Anyone...?)

All right. All right. I know. We were all just guessing at this point. Results weren't guaranteed, and there were a lot of ways this half-ass plan could sideways. Jesus take the wheel, because this time, we had to fool them. Really fool them, because we were out of ideas. There was no Plan G.

The snowmen were beating the tar out of Bubby. They were all over him. I hobbled out into the snow in my pink glitter high heels. Great. I was literally walking to my death in cheap plastic high heels. *Oh God. Nope. Can't do this. Can't.* My heart was Double Dutch jump roping in my rib cage.

I stopped. A pair of antennae emerged from Grandma Linda's wig.

"Aahhh!" I swatted at them.

"Hey, watch it, kid!" Kevin's face poked out of Grandma Linda's spare polyester hair.

"What are you doing?" I whispered.

"I couldn't let you go out here alone, kid," he said. "Okay. I admit when I first met you, I thought you were just another fat, lazy chickenshit millennial who wouldn't last three seconds."

"Gee, Kevin. Tell me how you really feel." If this was his final goodbye as I faced pending doom, he really should come up with a better speech.

"But you proved me wrong. I mean, yeah, you're fat," he said.

"Is this supposed to be a touching moment? I'm not feeling it."

"Shut up and let me talk," he said. "You're a good kid. When it comes down to it, you do the right thing even if it scares you. If you're gonna die, I'm not letting you do it alone. I'm gonna be right there with you."

Wait a minute. DIE? "Why did you send me out here if you didn't think this plan would work?"

"Someone had to do it. Besides, there's like a ten percent chance it'll work," Kevin said. "Have faith."

TEN PERCENT? That's it, I'm going back inside. I started to turn and nearly fell on my cheap glitter heel.

"Hold up, kid. It's worth a try. I did a quick Google search, and these guys weren't exactly Rhodes Scholars when they were alive," he said. "Just stick to the plan. Play dead. And don't forget: They need to see blood. Lots and lots of blood. Now, you got your armor on straight? You wearing a cup?"

Uh-oh. A cup. No. I forgot! Shoot. My nards!

And yes, Kevin said armor. I was wearing my pads from that one spring when I played—well, attempted to play, because I really sucked—lacrosse. I was fourteen. And calling it "armor" was definitely a stretch. I was about a hundred pounds lighter and a foot shorter then, so my chest pad now looked more like a bib. But it was hard, plastic, designed to take a hit, and was better than nothing. I wasn't about to go outside and let a bunch of evil snowman dickheads beat me without some protection, even if it was two sizes too small.

"Two sizes? Heh heh," Kevin said. "You wish. Keep telling yourself that, kid."

Shut up. You're not helping.

I slogged toward Caroline's Porsche. Bubby was next to the hood, fighting off angry snowmen. He was slicing and dicing them, even though they were just rolling themselves back together. He didn't intend to win. He was buying us time. When Bubby saw me, he put his claw-tipped pincer arms up, as if surrendering to the angry snowmen, then pointed at me and announced to the snowmen that "Behold! Your real target has arrived!"

Or something like that. It sounded more like bad gas. *Beerlp buurrrrr. Bleeeeeb wuuuuuuuuuuuurt.*

"Hit play!" Kevin said.

I pulled the phone out of my wet mink pocket just far enough to start the playlist DeeDee had cued up for me. She'd named it "Let the peasants drink Veuve Clicquot."

Boy. Was DeeDee was giving off a very strong French Revolution guillotine vibe for the holidays, or was it just me?

Caroline's voice sprang from my pocket, loud. DeeDee had turned the volume up to five zillion.

> "My daughter Madison Ford Vanderbilt is at Yale Law. She attended high school with your grandson, Lloyd," she said. "Well, I suppose working at a corner store is a success, considering his meager upbringing. You must be so proud."

My jaw dropped.

> "We come from a very good family. We know the value of hard work and frugality," a voice said. Grandma Mildred. "Lloyd was raised right."

My heart softened. Aw. Grandma Mildred had actually defended me. Maybe she was a little sweeter than a seasick crocodile after all.

> "It's not our fault he has chosen to be lazy and fat," she said.

All righty then. Scratch that. Grandma Mildred wasn't getting my kidney! DeeDee should have deleted that part. I didn't need to hear that.

"You got bigger problems, kid," Kevin said.

He was right. The decoy voice had worked. The snowmen had turned around. They were looking at me, up and down. It's like they were trying to decide if I was the real thing or another trick. Fool me twice, right?

"Get those hips swinging, kid," Kevin said.

Okay! Okay! I clopped slowly forward on my cheap plastic heels, thrusting my hips out with each step. The playlist cut to a new Caroline track.

> "My goodness, where did you buy that sweater? I've never seen anything so...*charming*. Why, if I didn't know better, I'd say it screams Home Shopping Network." Caroline guffawed. "My my. The things designers come up with. You certainly have to have a sense of humor if you're buying ready-to-wear. It's wonderful that there are so many kitsch options for those who can't afford couture."

> "Oh, this old thing? My personal shopper at Bergdorf picked it out for me. He was simply amazing, very in tune with Central Saint Martins. We flew him out for a closet styling on my private jet last summer. That was money well spent."

Man. This was like a Caroline Ford Vanderbilt greatest hits list.

> "Oh, my goodness. How can you stand yourself? I would never walk around with back rolls. Have you ever considered a Mommy makeover? They could fix you right up. Kiss those chicken flaps goodbye. They might even be able to liposuck you down a size or three. It's expensive, but you *might* be able to afford it if you have it done in Brazil."

DeeDee was right. Relaxation actually made her meaner. At least sober Caroline tried to disguise her insults as compliments.

"Incoming," Kevin yelled. "Stick to the plan, kid."

He retreated into Grandma's wig just as the first snowman attacked.

I was surrounded. They glared at me, charcoal briquette eyes in slits and mouths frowning. I had the nervous sweats so bad Kevin could have Slipped N Slid down my arms. The SnOSU snowman thwapped me right in the shin. I immediately dropped to my knees. *Ooooow!* Now I really didn't like Brutus the Buckeye. I mean, come on. Who thought a poisonous nut would make a good mascot? Seriously!

"Roll up, kid!" Kevin screeched in my ear.

And I did, full fetal position. I was so wrapped up, I was like a mink fur-covered Pokeball rolling around out in the snow.

Thwap. Thwap. Thwap. Thwap.

Good thing, too, because those snow creeps really laid into me. They hit and hit and they didn't stop, didn't let up, not even once.

Thwap. Thwap. Thwap. Thwap.

Holy crap. This really hurt. I covered my head with my arms.

Thwap. Thwap. Thwap. Thwap.

The faux Caroline playlist kept going.

> "Oh my. What is *this*? Is it edible? Well, I've never seen anything like that before. We're serving Almas caviar at the Legacy Dinner tonight. It's from albino Iranian sturgeon. Very exotic, very rare and *very* expensive. But, we said why not? We deserve to treat ourselves every once in a while. It's been such a hard year. Did you know the Winstons lost their beach house in the Caymans to a hurricane last summer? Such a tragedy. They only have two summer homes left. Poor things. Such a hardship."

Jesus. Was I seriously out here taking punches and putting my life on the line for this woman? She's literally the worst!

Thwap. Thwap. Thwap. Thwap.

Eeow. Eeow. Eeow. Eeow. My back burned, like someone had poured boiling water all over it. Why did getting hit with sticks hurt so bad?

"It's called caning, kid," Kevin said. "It's no tickle party. Just ask the Indonesians."

What are you even talking about?

"You'd know if you read books."

Thwap. Thwap. Thwap. Thwap.

They thrashed me across the head. And *Thump. Thump. Thump.* Holy crap. A couple of them must have added icy feet to their bodies when they reformed because they were kicking me!

"Owwwww!" I screamed.

"Turn the moans up an octave, kid," Kevin said. "You're supposed to be a lady in pain, not a dude."

I wanted to tell him to shut up, but my all of me hurt too badly. I fell over, into the snow and held tight to my knees, tucking my head as deeply into the coat and into Grandma's wig as I could.

Thwap. Thwap. Thwap. Thwap.

Eowch. My stomach clenched up and my mouth watered. The pain was so sharp I was pretty sure I was gonna vomit. They didn't let up. These guys never got tired, did they?

Thwap. Thwap. Thwap. Thwap.

Something ran down my face, stinging my skin. It burned when it hit my lips. I licked the corner of my mouth. *Crap. Diablo sauce!* And a snow creep had just thwapped some of it into my eye. *Blink. Blink. Nope. Stay out! Holy crap. Too late. Aaaaaaaaaah!* My eyeball was ON FIRE! Okay, not technically on fire, but it hurt so so so so so bad. I whimpered. This sucked so hard.

Caroline's voice was still chattering out of my pocket, going on and on about how Prada was so last year and Hermes never goes out of style. "I just got my third Birkin bag, by the way. You really *have* to know someone."

"Turn it off, kid! Turn it off!" Kevin screamed in my ear. "Dying women don't talk about fashion! You'll blow it!"

Uh, I'd seen Caroline badly injured, and she did in fact talk about fashion. She had wailed over a Prada tennis shoe while her leg was broken in ten places. But still, point taken. I really didn't want to move my arm, which was wrapped around my head, protecting it from possessed snow monsters. On Christmas Eve. (Jesus, how did this become my life?) But I knew I had to flip off the playlist. Kevin was right.

"Cover the sound. Moan, kid. Louder!"

I did. *Eooooooooooooow!*

I sounded like a wounded werewolf. I didn't have to try hard to moan, because dude. These snowmen really knew how to throw a punch. And did I mention my eyeball was ON FIRE? Who the hell put the Diablo packs *in the wig*???

"Higher voice, kid!"

I dialed it up. *Eooooooooooooow!* Okay, now I sounded like a wounded Britney Spears singing "Werewolves of London."

I managed to work my hand down to my pocket and flip off the playlist. *Phew.*

Ack! The cost was a coconut bra across the cheek. *Eeeeeaaaaaaaa!*

It cut like a razor. A splurp of warm liquid dripped down my cheek. *Shit. It's blood. Real blood!*

"It's time, kid," Kevin whispered. He was right in my ear, like an FBI surveillance wire, his antennae tickling all the bits. "Play dead. Now! Make it good."

Thank God. I was ready for this to be over. I flipped into full ham it up, high school musical, Shakespeare in the damn park mode. I drew in a loud deep breath, rolled slightly forward onto my stomach, planted my face in the snow and splayed my arms out. *"Uuuuuuuuuuuuuuuuuuuuuuh."*

That was my approximation of a death rattle. I let out a very long, low breath, as if all the air and life had rolled right out of me.

It must have been convincing, because the snowmen only thwapped me, oh, maybe five or six more excruciating times, and not as enthusiastically. Those thwaps were more like when you shoot a zombie for a second time just to be *sure* sure it's dead.

Phew. They stopped.

I couldn't see what they were doing though, because I was face down in snow trying really really hard to stay stone dead still.

"Attaaaaaaaaaaaaaaaaaaaaaack!"

Uh. Who the hell just yelled "attack?" The voice was way too high to be DeeDee or Doc, and Bubby didn't speak English.

"Here comes trouble," Kevin whispered. "It's that dipshit kid. What's his name?"

Scooter?

"Yeah, that one."

What's he doing?

"Mucking up the plan."

"Hi ya! Hi ya!" Scooter screamed.

I heard the flat, muted *cuuuuush cuuuuush* sound of something hitting snow. A sprinkle of cold powder landed on the back of my neck, melting straight down into my shirt like an ice flow. *Brrrr. This sucks!*

"Scooter used a wooden baseball bat to knock the head off that snowman in the Hawaiian shirt," Kevin said. "The snowman doesn't look too happy about it, but I won't know for sure until his head stops rolling. Oh. Wait. Yeah. He's mad."

Dammit Scooter! Why is he outside?

"Oh, shit. The kid's in trouble. The snowmen are after him. And he can totally see them moving. Heh heh. Kid's gonna have nightmares tonight, for sure."

After him? Well, hell. I couldn't let the snowmen get Scooter. No matter how much I hated him, he was only nine.

"Better run, kid!" Kevin said.

Can they see me? Are they looking this way?

"Who?"

The snowmen, duh. Who else?

"Nah. They're chasing the kid. He's putting up a good fight though."

I rolled onto my side just enough so I could see. The snowmen were inching toward Scooter, leaving trails in the snow behind them. They had their stick arms puffed out, like they were pumped up wrestlers waiting to make a move. They looked even scarier, because the bursting ketchup and corn syrup packs made them look like they were splattered in real blood. And Scooter. Man, that kid must be in Little League or something, because he was swinging that bat like he was Barry Bonds. Not that it mattered. He could bust them apart all day long. They'd just reform.

"I gotta help him." I started to get up.

"Don't move, kid. You'll blow it! We've got a house full of people to save. Your job is to lie there and play dead. Don't mess it up."

I can't let them hurt Scooter. He's a kid.

"The kid's a jerk. Although he's a good hitter. I'll give him that. But you need to stay put."

Just then, the front door opened and DeeDee stepped out.

"See? She's got it covered."

"Wait. The snowmen think I'm dead. Why are they still here? Why didn't they get de-possessed or whatever?"

"How am I supposed to know? Maybe the kid mucked it up. Maybe they need revenge on him now, too. Either way, don't overthink it. Stop moving and play dead."

I did stop moving, because I thought DeeDee was on her way to help Scooter. But she was so slow. She was lumbering. Her arms were full of—I had to squint, because one eye was blurry thanks to all the Diablo sauce—but I swear she had a plate of cookies in one hand, a twelve pack of Natural Light Strawberry Lemonade tucked under her arm, and two bottles of whiskey in her other hand. What was she doing? We needed help!

"Hi ya! Jerk!" Scooter's bat cut my beefed-up (now topless, because it'd beaten me with the coconut bra and hadn't bothered to put it back on) Florida-or-bust lady snowman. Snow person? Whatever. Anyway, Scooter batted that thing right in half. Chunks of grass skirt flew through the air, green plastic shimmering in the moonlight. It's top half thwumped straight to the ground. Scooter proceeded to *thwump thwump*

thwump beat the crap out of it with his bat, crunching it down to nothing. He was so angry and so determined to beat it to pulp that the other snowmen leaned back a little and looked at each other like "WTF?"

I know, right? Kid's got anger issues.

"Ha. Take that, Lloyd!" Scooter growled. "You're not gonna win MY trophy this year. It's mine! Mine! Mine! Mine!"

He punctuated each "Mine" with another thunk of his bat against snowman body.

OMG, are you hearing this? Scooter was staring down thirteen haunted demon snowmen, and all he cared about was winning the snowman contest. Oh, he was going down. I wasn't sure how, but I'd figure it out.

"You were gonna help *him*?" Kevin said. "The kid's a maniac!"

True. All true. But I still couldn't sentence him to death by snow creep. They had clearly gotten over their initial shock, because they were moving closer and closer to Scooter, who was clutching his bat, telling them that if they didn't stop, he wasn't afraid to use it. But I could see the terror in his eyes, as his third-grade brain wrapped around the fact that the snowmen were alive. And supernatural. And, they weren't the sweet, Burl Ives, happy, singing *Rudolph the Red-Nosed Reindeer* Rankin and Bass Christmas special kind of snowmen. I wiggled, trying to get some leverage to sit up.

"Don't move a muscle, kid. You'll blow it!"

"Dead Caroline wasn't enough, or they'd be gone by now."

"Stop. Fine. Hand me the phone. Let me call Doc. He'll tell us what to do. Then you can get up."

"We don't have time for that."

FWUMP.

Or maybe we did.

Because Bubby's big blue jelly tail had just flattened all the snowmen like they were junk cars at a monster truck rally. All but one. The one he missed was so sick of Bubby that he was now climbing him like a tree. Man, he could really move those possessed twig arms. They were still twigs, so they weren't particularly bendy, which made the whole scene extra creepy. He moved like a mechanical spider, scaling Bubby's claw-tipped legs, fast and angry, then hopping right up onto Bubby's face. The snow creep was punching. And Bubby was swinging his head, roaring, trying to pry him off.

Scooter stood still and silent as if he'd been turned into a Popsicle. A yellow pool was forming in the snow around his boots. *Aw, man!* He'd peed himself. Of course he had. He had watched *something* smoosh a bunch of evil dead snowmen. And he was now watching a creepy spider snowman swinging around in (what looked to Scooter to be) thin air, twenty feet off the ground. He was too scared to scream. His little brain was probably short circuiting under his Scooby Doo sock cap.

Plup. Plup. Plup.

Uh oh. I looked up. Yep. That was the sound of my Dad's carefully placed Christmas lights popping out of their clips. He'd gone full on Clark Griswold with the lights this year. And Bubby was so busy trying to shake the snowman off his face, he had accidentally bumped the roof and gotten a few of his claw-tipped centipede arms caught in the multicolored light strings. The lights flickered, but stayed on.

Please stay on! PLEASE! Seriously. My Mom could only handle so much Christmas disaster in one night. The Christmas tree had fallen over. Gertrude had peed out the lights. A window had broken. Brooke wasn't coming home tonight. This was shaping up to be Mom's nightmare Christmas. I could not let this get any worse. We had to save the day! But, as a real Magic 8-Ball would say, "Outlook not so good."

Bubby was fighting that snow creep hard, swinging and twirling around. The harder he fought, the more light clips popped off.

Plup. Plup. Plup.

A dozen light strings wrapped around him, and they were starting to slow him down.

Kevin was calling Doc, but Doc wasn't answering. Kevin insisted I lie in the snow like a wet, dead mink-clad Sasquatch, powerless to help anyone, watching this Christmas shit show hit the North Pole's biggest fan. But I wasn't sure how much longer I could just lie here. The snow creeps Bubby had smooshed were already reforming around Scooter. Disembodied heads and torsos rolled around and around in the snow, rolling themselves back together, pulling twigs and charcoal and scarves and carrot noses back into themselves. Scooter watched, too scared to scream.

DeeDee was *setting up a picnic?* What the hell? She'd laid a blanket on the ground and had arranged the beer, the whiskey and cookies on it. Okay. I don't remember this being part of the plan, do you?

The phone rang and rang. Kevin had it on speaker. "Ten bucks says he's not answering because he's second basing it with Grandma Hot to Trot."

Shut up, Kevin!

"Hello, bug man," Doc said.

"Plan ain't working," Kevin said.

"Yes. It is. We have broken the code. They were vengeful ghosts *and* lemures. The Pocket Guide did not mislead us. DeeDee will close the spell."

"What do I do with the kid?"

"He must lie still and pretend to be dead. At all costs," Doc said. "I must go, bug man. The big fine woman is waiting."

Then he hung up.

"I told you so," he said to me.

Shut up!

Bubby was now completely wrapped, head to toe, in my Dad's Christmas lights, twinkling in the falling snow like the tree at Rockefeller Center. Except much more jiggly. And fighting a snow demon. Until, fed up, Bubby reared his head back, stabbed that creepy snowman with two pincers, then threw him splat onto the ground.

Scooter screamed. He was staring at Bubby. Like he could *see* Bubby. *Oh shit.* The magic bag of hippy invisibility crystals was tangled up in the snow creep's twig arm.

This wasn't good. Not good at all.

The snow creep shook off the fall and rejoined the other twelve snowmen, who were now closing in on one very terrified Scooter.

Nope. I couldn't just lie here. This was a disaster. I moved, and Kevin bit down hard on my ear.

OWWWW! What, did roaches have vampire teeth? That hurt!

"Doc said don't move, kid," he said. "If you blow it, we all die, and I have to stop drinking. You will not like me if my Christmas buzz wears off. Trust me."

"But Kevin. We're losing!"

"Doc said it's handled, it's handled. Relax."

"It sure doesn't look like it's handled!"

Bubby was now wrapped so tight in the lights that he was practically tethered to the side of the house. He wiggled and jiggled, trying to break free, but that only knotted the light strings up more. We couldn't count on Bubby to help again anytime soon. And did I mention *he was no longer fucking invisible?*

My blood was pumping so hard it was pounding my temples like a gong. *Oh my God. Yep. I'm having a heart attack.*

DeeDee, was way too cazh, surveying her picnic spread like the world wasn't completely unraveling around us. She shook her head, dissatisfied. Then she pulled a bottle of Jack Daniels out of her coat pocket and arranged it on the blanket just so. What was she Martha Stewart? Hello? Snow creeps! Anyone?

Scooter clung to his baseball bat, white knuckled. His eyes were as round as dinner plates. The snowmen were closing in.

Okay then. So please join me *again* in Christmas prayer. * clears throat *

Dear Baby Jesus, I know I said bad things about Scooter, and I wished bad things would happen to him, but let the record show that I did not want him to die. I did not want a bunch of blood-thirsty snowmen to kill him. He's only nine. I know you're busy, Scooter's a total dickhead, and it's your birthday, but if you could throw me a Hail Mary, I'd really appreciate it.

"Geesh, kid. Have a little faith," Kevin said.

"I am. That's why I'm praying."

"In us, dumbass." Kevin shook his head. "See? Watch the lady work."

Sure enough, DeeDee grabbed Scooter right as the first set of twig arms nearly thwapped down on him. She scooped him up, threw him two feet backward into a soft pile of snow, and stepped in front of him. She took the hits that were meant for him. More twig arms thwap thwapped down on her, but she batted them off like she was freaking Wonder Woman.

A handful of the snowmen, clearly frustrated, jumped up and arced through the air like super-powered movie villains, preparing to strike down hard. That's when DeeDee did a kung fu windmill move with her arms, and small brown throwing stars shot through the air, thunking straight into snowman faces. The snowmen all went down, one by one.

Yes! Go DeeDee! But, man. I was out of breath just watching her. How did she do all that ninja stuff?

"She goes to the gym. You should, too," Kevin said. "Seriously, kid. You're really letting yourself go."

Shut up, Kevin.

"Don't shoot the messenger," he said.

Then the snowmen bent down before her, like they were on one knee. Their heads were down.

Crunch. Crunch. Crunch.

Wait. Did you hear that?

Crunch. Crunch. Crunch.

The snowmen's heads were vibrating. No, moving, like they were chewing? What had she just thrown at them?

DeeDee opened the *Pocket Guide to Monstrous Creatures* and ran her finger down a page, taking her sweet time. I wanted to scream, "Run, DeeDee, run!" It was only a matter of time before they attacked again.

We'd learned that much. But Kevin made me stay quiet.

She said, reading aloud, "Nos autem immolandum victimas suas coram iratus spirituum."

Seriously? When will these people learn to stop reading these damned books out loud?

"At least she's reading," Kevin said.

Shut up!

"I'll shut up when you read your employee manual."

Crunch. Crunch. Crunch.

It was the snowmen. And they were definitely chewing. I could see their little snow jaws working up and down.

Mmmmmmm. Mmmmmmm. Mmmmmmm.

And now they were making yummy noises? What was going on here? So confused.

And when I thought it couldn't get weirder, they sat up, like dogs begging for treats. Well, if those dogs had gaping black holes for mouths. Jesus. Their faces looked just like the ghastly guy in that book. *What the?*

DeeDee took a handful of whatever she'd thrown at them before and tossed them, one by one, into the snowmen's mouths. They chomped down and made happy yum sounds. *Mmmm mmmm mmmmm.* She tossed the last one and as it tumbled through the air, I could see it was a gingerbread ninja, turning head over heel, right into a possessed snowman's mouth.

Angel eight ball rolled out from behind Caroline's back tire and hit me right in the nose. "You better hope DeeDee got the words right because if Grandma Mildred dies tonight, I can't guarantee she's going through heaven's gate," triangle said. "You definitely need to buy her a little more time to turn her life around. <hiccup>"

Oh. Great. No pressure.

"Wonderful job, guys. Really, bravo." DeeDee began to clap. The snowmen looked at each other. "You deserve a round of applause. That lady was a total bitch. Thank you so much for killing her. Look what you have done. Mission accomplished. Good work everyone."

She pointed at me. Okay, to dead Caroline.

"Play dead, kid. NOW!" Kevin screamed.

I flopped back down in the snow and stayed stone still. And nothing happened. Not right away. A minute or two later, I heard a strange noise like twigs knocking together. Then a *crusssss crussss crusss* of snowman butt scooting through fresh-fallen snow.

What's happening up there?

"DeeDee is aces, that's what," Kevin said. "They bought it. The dipshits totally bought it!"

How can you be so sure?

"Because I'm watching them all sit around having a damn picnic, drinking whiskey, and high-fiving each other because you—oh, excuse me—Caroline is freakin' dead. Man. This is definitely one for the books."

No way. I swiveled my head and opened one eye. Sure enough, they were on that blanket, taking swigs right out of the whiskey bottles, passing them around. They did this for what seemed like forever, but really was only long enough to drain a twelve-pack of Natural Light and one bottle of Wild Turkey. Then DeeDee said, "Ope. Sorry, guys. Looks like your ride is here." She pointed up the court to the ambulance. "You better catch them. Don't let them leave without you."

They looked up at the red and white lights, still flashing. They each took one last shot of whiskey.

"Enjoy it, because there won't be anything good to drink where y'all are going," Kevin whispered.

The snowmen cracked opened a bottle of Jack Daniels. Then, each of them took a swig and passed the bottle. As soon as the bottle left its hand, the snow creep stopped moving. One by one, they froze, and the eerie orange light drained out of them.

Woosh. A red streak, fast as lightning, zipped through the air.

"It's safe to get up now, Lloyd," DeeDee said. "It's over."

I rolled over, face to the sky, just in time to watch the red streak zip straight through the ambulance door. The truck then drove away, disappearing over the horizon. The bodies—and their spirits—bagged and tagged in the back.

"What did you say to those guys?" Kevin asked her.

"Oh, you know, something about humbly making a sacrifice to the angry spirits? Apparently, lemures need to eat to realize they are dead. They won't cross over on an empty stomach," DeeDee said. "Maybe they died hungry. Who knows? Either way, dinner and revenge was the magic formula."

DeeDee was a genius. A smart, beautiful, dead-language reading genius. And thanks to her, this was over. I took a long, deep breath. Christmas was saved. Time to relax. Hellz yeah.

"Hold that thought," Kevin said.

The front door flew open. A drunk, happy Big Dan ran out into the court.

"Hey guys. What are you doing?"

He looked at me. "Why are you dressed like that?"

Then at DeeDee and her snowman picnic. "Oh, cool. You got the snowmen ready. Good thing, too. Everyone's getting their coats on. They'll be out in a minute. We decided to judge the contest early, because we're supposed to get twenty more inches of snow tonight and the oldsters are worried the snowmen will be buried if we wait."

I swear my heart stopped beating, and my blood pressure dropped to zero. On their way OUTSIDE???

"Shit! Shit! Shit!" Kevin screamed. "The coat!"

He didn't need to tell me. I hopped up, stripped off Caroline's coat, and chucked it through one of the busted-out windows of her Porsche. It thunked, covered in food coloring and taco sauce, onto her front seat.

"The wig!" Kevin said.

Shoot! I took that off and chucked it under the back tire. I didn't want to implicate Grandma Linda in the vandalism of Caroline's car. If we'd learned anything about Caroline Ford Vanderbilt, it was that she liked revenge and lawsuits.

DeeDee was distracting Big Dan, smiling and telling him about our boozy snowman picnic like it was a joke, and we had planned it all for the contest. Genius.

He didn't seem to notice the two-story tall jelly hell centipede furiously trying to free himself from the Christmas lights.

"Chooooooooooooooooooooooooooooooooooooooooo!"

So of course, Bubby sneezed. Yep. Just my luck.

It was so long, so low, the world shook. Big Dan looked up, saw Bubby, who was still strapped to the house with Christmas lights, and screamed, "AAAAAAAAAAAAAAAAAAAAAAAAAAAHHHHHHHHH! WHAT THE FUCK IS THAT?"

Then, Big Dan passed out cold from fear. I mean, he fainted like a Victorian lady and landed face down in the snow.

I looked at DeeDee and said "Bubby!" As in, "how are we going to hide him?"

I could hear voices gathering at the door. The neighbors. The guests. My parents!! About to step outside.

DeeDee lunged toward the snowman who'd ripped Bubby's charm bag off, but the stupid thing must have been stuck in his twig hands, because she was wrestling with it pretty hard and it didn't seem to be moving.

Bubby, with his few remaining free claws started shaking snow off the roof and up off the ground so furiously there was an icy cloud all around him. I mean, he was Edward Scissorhanding that shit. Snow was flying. What was he doing?

Too late. My Mom stepped out first. "Where have you been, honey? Are you wearing lipstick?"

Crap! I furiously rubbed my mouth with the sleeve of Great Aunt Edna's sweater. I'm pretty sure the lipstick came right off, along with all my skin, because that wool was like a cheese grater.

"Oh my. What do we have here?" Mom said. She walked over to DeeDee's snowman picnic. "Is this what you kids have been working on? I wondered where you all had gotten off to!"

A gigantic clump of neighbors, totally tipsy, now stood on the lawn laughing over DeeDee's snowman picnic. They stepped right over Big Dan to take a closer look. Huh. Maybe they thought he was part of the display? Who could say?

Scooter saw his parents and ran to them, screaming. "A monster! There's a monster! Look! Look!" He hid behind them and pointed at Bubby.

Dammit, Scooter! How was I going to explain this? My mind reeled. Jig's up. World spinning.

Everyone looked up at Bubby. I did, too.

Oh. My. God. I couldn't believe my eyes. Bubby was a genius. Now all that Edward Scissorhands crap made sense. That cloud of flying flakes? Camouflage. His body was covered tip to tail in a light dusting of snow, just enough to obscure his blue jelly body with a shimmering white sheen. He stood absolutely still, wrapped in twinkling lights. He looked like a gigantic fat two-story tall snowman. Okay, yeah, a snowman with a weirdly shaped body, but still. He was totally rocking it. The twinkling lights strings strapped around him only added to the look.

Scooter's parents turned to the panicking and screaming third grader and said, "See, silly? That's not a monster, that's a snowman. Isn't it wonderful?"

In fact, everyone was staring at Bubby, marveling. They bought the ruse, and they were totally eating it up. Everyone except Scooter, who was flipping out.

And Grandma Mildred who took one step outside, looked at the snowman picnic and at Bubby and said, "Really, Jennifer. What is this nonsense? You actually spend money on trophies to hand out for this? How wasteful. No wonder you can't afford to live in a nice neighborhood."

Thump. Yep. You heard that. That was the sound of Bubby hitting the porch roof, which unleashed a mini avalanche of snow that fell right onto Grandma Mildred's head. Her head and face were totally covered in wet white snow. Her open mouth—agape in shock—kinda made her look like a Muppet yeti. Well, that shut her up.

My Mom slogged through the snow, right on over to me. She pinched my cheek. "You kids. So creative! I'm so proud of you, Lloyd.

This means so much to me. You really went out of your way to make this party special."

She had no idea.

CHAPTER 16

Ding.

The clock in the living room chimed. One a.m. It was officially Christmas. The last of the house guests had stumbled home an hour ago. Mom and Dad were in bed, upstairs, happily sleeping off their buzz. Grandma Mildred and Great Aunt Edna were camped out in Brooke's room, likely ruminating about the snow incident and their ungrateful family. (Okay, I was guessing, but it was a pretty good guess. At least Great Aunt Edna had stopped knitting. You're welcome, world.) I could hear the gentle *zzzzzzzzzzzz* of Grandpa Eugene, still asleep in the armchair in the living room.

We were in the den. Angel eight ball lay in my lap, silent, sleeping off his buzz. The *Pocket Guide to Monstrous Creatures* lay on the footstool, curled up with Gertrude. They were both purring. DeeDee sat next to me on the sofa, wrapped in a fuzzy blanket, glass of tapioca in her hand, smiling. Yes, I said tapioca. Apparently, angel eight ball had missed a bottle.

Kevin sat on the microphone, cueing up the karaoke machine. The top quarter of Bubby's body was jammed in through the sliding door. Bubby had a microphone as well and was waiting for the music to start. He had a Santa hat balanced precariously on the top of his head, his magic necklace was tied firmly in place, and three of his claw arms held cups of eggnog. He clutched a golden trophy proudly to his chest (Carapace? Ugh. Whatever). First place. Best Snowman. He had earned it.

I took a swig of my eggnog, and my phone buzzed. Big Dan. Again. Mrs. Miller had peeled him out of the snow and taken him home. He'd called or texted me at least a dozen times since, asking about the big blue bug in the yard. "What should I tell him?"

"Tell him it was the pot brownie," she said.

"Good plan." I typed that out, adding, "That weed probably had something weird in it."

Send.

What? Big Dan had to buy it. I mean, if I hadn't taken a hit of Big Dan's weird weed before I went to get that slushy, I never would have gotten the job at Demon Mart in the first place. I would have taken one look at that tentacle monster, realized it was real, and run far far away.

If I had, I would have a normal life, a normal Christmas Eve. Then again, I wouldn't have DeeDee. Or, a talking roach getting ready to rock out on the karaoke machine, or a giant hell centipede poking in through my back door, all smiles.

Or Caroline Ford Vanderbilt passed out face down on the shag rug next to the television, dead to the world. She had bits of chip dip and cheese puff stuck in her hair, lipstick streaked across her face, and no idea she was about to be serenaded badly by hell beasts. Turns out, she'd hit the alcohol and muscle relaxers a little too hard, and had actually managed to roofy herself. It was probably for the best. Her Porsche was still bumper-deep in snow, with busted out windows and a totally destroyed mink coat in the seat, but you know what? We'd deal with it tomorrow. We'd tell her vandals, hooligans, did it. We wouldn't technically be lying.

"I don't see any Dio on the playlist, kid," Kevin said, messing with the controls.

"Uh, sorry. There's no Dio on there."

Kevin shook his head. "I taught you better than that, kid," he said. "Oh well. This'll do."

Kevin typed some numbers into the karaoke machine and a black screen with purple lyrics popped up on the television. "Prepare to be wowed."

A piano intro poured from the speakers. Kevin flipped on the disco ball and pointed his top leg at DeeDee. He sang to her about how she was a small-town girl in a lonely world.

Holy shit. Kevin can really sing!

Bubby sang too, adding a low bass blurble to Kevin's surprisingly good rendition of "Don't Stop Believin'." They air guitared the solo together, and they totally rocked it. Maybe it was all the extra legs, or something about being a bug, but they were amazingly great at that.

"Don't look so surprised, kid," Kevin said during the interlude. "I was in a band back in the day."

No way. Kevin looked at me. I looked at him. What? He's a roach. How was that even possible?

Suddenly, eight ball jumped straight up out of my lap and hovered in the air for a hot minute before dropping straight back down into my crotch. *Thud.*

Ouch.

He rolled, window up. "I win."

"Win what?"

"Doc and Grandma are in the laundry room. Third base! Who's getting a new harp? This guy!"

Nope. Didn't hear that. Lalalalalalalalala.

The song ended. We all clapped and hooted. DeeDee dug another peppermint stick out of her Santa bag and tossed it to Bubby, who opened his mouth and buzz-sawed it down to sugar powder in two seconds flat. Then, she raised her glass to us. "I don't know about you, but all my Christmas wishes definitely came true," she said. "This was the best Christmas ever."

The End

Thank you SO much for reading Hell for the Holidays and the 24/7 Demon Mart series. Visit me at Dmguay.com to stay up to date on all the latest Demon Mart news!

WHO THE HECK IS DM GUAY?

D. M. Guay writes about the intersection of real life with the supernatural. She's an award-winning journalist living in Ohio, a hobby urban farmer (you can't beat her beets!), a painter, and a retired roller derby player. Her favorite things—besides books— are tiki bars, liquid eyeliner, the 1968 Camaro, 24-hour horror movie festivals, art by Picasso, rock concerts, and most of all, people who make art, despite adversity, no matter what life throws at them.

Half the profits from her annual book sales go to research for kidney cancer treatments and cures. She has stage 4 kidney cancer and is still alive and kicking eighteen months *after* her oncologist said she would be dead. Thanks for reading. Visit her at www.dmguay.com, follow her on Bookbub, or visit her at twitter.com/dmguay.

Made in the USA
Middletown, DE
31 May 2020